I0534536

All Things Considered

SISTERHOOD CHRONICLES 5

ANITA DAVIS

This is a work of fiction. Names, characters, businesses, places, events and incidents are either the products of the author's imagination or used in a fictitious manner. Any resemblance to actual persons, living or dead, or actual events is purely coincidental.

Copyright © 2018 Anita Davis

All Rights Reserved. No part of this publication may be reproduced, stored in a retrieval system, or transmitted, in any form or in any means – by electronic, mechanical, photocopying, recording or otherwise – without prior written permission.

ISBN-10: 1-946721-08-5
ISBN-13: 978-1-946721-08-2

Books may be purchased in quantity by contacting the author Anita Davis:
Set Apart Publishing
PO Box 39229
Chicago, IL 60639
or by email at authoranitadavis@gmail.com

DEDICATION

Thank you, God, for helping me pull it together long enough to finish this book.

Between my reading binges, work, and workouts, it was a great feat to finally finish this book. LBS.

Writing this book is credited to a reader, who, after I released Kim's story on a Saturday, left a review on that Sunday saying how much she enjoyed Kim's story and hopefully there was more to be told about the Sisterhood.

I had planned to end the series with Kim's story but my readers and my imagination prompted and promoted this book.

This is for you all. I hope you each enjoy it.

Life is not linear. You can experience your happiness while others experience theirs.

~Anita Davis

1

Renee

Rain pellets slapped the large window pane in Renee's room. The sky mirrored how she felt, gloomy.

She sniffled and wiped her face before she repositioned her head on the pillow. She hadn't slept this many nights in her old room at her parents' house since she had first returned from school in D.C. That was before she secured her job with the Department of Children and Family Services and moved out on her own. She definitely hadn't cried as much as she had since her days with Ted, but given Kim's funeral was just the week before, crying had become her constant.

Thinking she needed time alone to come to terms with her sissy being gone, she tried going home after the funeral, but the silence was too much for her. She sat in the dark for hours waiting on Kim to either call her or show up at her house unannounced. But night soon turned into morning, which brought her more mourning after waking up with a splitting headache and checking her phone to see no missed calls or texts from Kim.

Being alone at home didn't seem to be helping her much, so she camped out at her parent's house.

Aside from sitting on the couch mindlessly watching TV with Andrew a few days that week or snuggled under either her mother or father, she found shelter in the room she once shared with Kim.

They grew up in a five-bedroom house, enough rooms for Renee to have had her own, separate bedroom from Kim when they were younger, but the sisters ensured their parents they wanted to bunk together.

Staying in the room the past week since the funeral both comforted and saddened Renee. Kim's old cheerleading memorabilia and New Edition posters on the walls made Renee feel close to her. Seeing it all brought back fond memories of their grammar and high school years, but then looking over at Kim's made up twin bed knowing it would never be occupied by her again, kept the tears flowing.

There was a knock at the door.

"Come in," Renee said, barely above a whisper.

The door slowly creaked open and Monica peeked her head in. "It's us, sweetie. Can we come in?"

"Sure." Renee cleared her throat.

Monica walked in first, but Pam was close on her heels. They made their way to Renee's bed near the window, but each stared briefly at Kim's unoccupied bed before emotions forced them to look away.

"Renee, how are you?" Pam came from behind Monica but stood next to her. They hovered near her bed and stared at Renee's back for a second before she finally rolled over and looked at them.

"Good and not good." Her tears quickened their pace down her face and her chest began to heave up and down.

"Oh, Renee." Monica dropped her purse on the floor and squatted to embrace Renee.

Renee sat up, making it easier for Monica to put her arms around her, and she soon felt Pam's touch and could hear her wispy cries in her ear.

"It's understandable, but we'll get through this together," Monica said, squeezing Renee.

Pam pulled away from her friends in search of a box of Kleenex. She grabbed the lavender, floral design box from the nightstand, adjacent to Renee's bed, and returned to her friends' embrace. She divided tissue between the three of them.

After their cries subsided, they all seemed to direct their attention to Kim's empty bed.

"I just can't believe she's gone." Renee shook her head.

"Me, either." Pam rubbed Renee's back.

Monica dabbed at her face with the tissue.

The reality of what day of the week it was settled in with Renee and she turned her attention back to her dearest friends of over two decades. "It's Thursday, what are you two doing here this time of day?"

"Vance had to get back to Jensen this week since he's the principal and had meetings he just couldn't reschedule to a later date, but I just haven't been able to gather myself enough to be in the classroom with my students yet. I tried going in yesterday and about halfway through my second-period class, I found myself bawling while writing something on the board," Pam said.

Renee began to dab at the tears streaming Pam's face.

"I looked at the clock and realized it was about the time Kim would be walking her students to one of their specials like gym or music. She would've stuck her head in my room and said something sassy to me to make the kids laugh and me shoo her out of the room. I cried until I felt Vance's arms around me.

"A student ran and got him. He had come up with a sub, had me to gather my things, and took me home.

He stayed with me for as long as he could before he had to get back for an afterschool meeting. When he came back home, we talked and agreed that I just stay out for the rest of the week and even longer if need be."

"I guess it helps when your husband is the boss," Monica quipped.

Pam chuckled. "Whatever! My husband may be my boss, but being your own boss is even better."

"Yes, it is." Monica cleared her throat. "You know I have a team of people under me to entrust the events I plan to if ever I'm absent for an event. I have dealt with a lot in life, low self-esteem, thinking I would never have kids, and almost refusing your brother's hand in marriage," she looked into Renee's slanted eyes, "but losing Kim has floored me. Feels like I've been gutted by the reality that I no longer have one of my best friends with me, that she won't help me raise the twins or this baby." Monica rubbed her stomach, although she was only a little under two months and hadn't begun to show yet. "So being my own boss has really benefitted me this week. I'm just grateful for a great staff, understanding clients, and you all." She leaned in to hug Pam and Renee again.

"Speaking of the twins, where are they?" Renee asked as she pulled back from her friends.

"You don't hear them?" Monica asked.

They quieted themselves and soon heard the infectious laughter of the twins playing with their grandparents.

"You know I can't dare set foot in this house without them. Your parents would have a fit." Monica snickered.

"Yeah, they would. And how is that brother of mine doing?" Renee asked.

Monica sighed. "My husband, Keith?"

"Yes, he's my only brother." Renee gave Monica a knowing look.

"He's back to work."

"Back to work?" Pam asked, wide-eyed.

"Yeah, he says it's the only thing keeping him sane. I lost one of my best friends, but he lost his triplet sister. Losing Kim was like losing one third of his heart." She sighed again. "We're both grieving and everybody grieves in different ways." Monica wiped her eyes.

Renee's gaze returned to Kim's empty bed. She took a deep breath trying to will herself not to go into a crying fit again.

"Yes, we all grieve differently. While losing Kim hurts me to the core and has shattered my being, knowing I'll be meeting my son tomorrow face to face for the first time since I gave him up at birth, has kept me from completely falling apart. I guess. It's like I can be right in the middle of a breakdown and thoughts of meeting him come to mind and somehow comfort me for a while, before the fear of how he'll respond to me takes over." Renee covered her face with her hands.

Pam rubbed her back. "Oh, sweetie, you should be excited about meeting him and not fear whether or not he'll like you. We'd be hard-pressed to find someone who doesn't, but that's another reason why Monica and I really believe that we should go with you to D.C. Be there with you when you meet him."

"Yeah, Renee. We wanna be there to support you," Monica chimed in. "Be there with you like how we all know Kim would."

Renee chuckled through her tears. She squeezed each of their hands. "I know you all do and I'm so grateful to have such supportive friends. The sisterhood is still very special to me, but this is something I have to do on my own."

"But Andrew is going with you, isn't he?" Monica said with a hint of jealousy in her voice.

"Yes." Renee found her smile. "Yes, he is. He wants to be there with me, and please don't take this the wrong way you guys, but I want him to be there, too." Renee's eyes widened, hoping her friends would understand her. She pulled her legs, covered by her long jean skirt, up to her chest and perched her chin on her knees. She really hoped her friends understood her choice for her journey.

"I guess so," Pam said.

"Yeah, yeah," Monica mumbled, then smiled.

"Thank you, guys, so much." Renee lurched forward and flung her arms around both of them, pulling them in for a tight hug.

"Let's pray for safe travels, open hearts, and a great reunion," Pam said.

"Thanks," Renee said and bowed her head as Pam led the prayer.

Moments later they stood up from the bed with tears streaming their faces from the heartfelt prayers they each prayed aloud.

Monica cleared her throat and looked at Renee. "You just better be glad we're not as audacious as Kim was, otherwise we'd get on that plane with you tomorrow whether you liked it or not."

They all found themselves looking over at Kim's empty bed one last time before they squeezed each other's hands and walked out of the room together with their heads low.

2

Renee

Renee had just finished unpacking her suitcase when there was a knock at her hotel door.

"Just a minute," she said as she stopped at the floor length mirror on the wall and made sure her hair was smoothed down. Since she had been dating Andrew, she found herself making sure she was more kempt than what she used to before him.

She pulled the door opened and smiled at how he smiled at her. His almost black, piercing eyes always seemed to widen with admiration for her.

"Hello, beautiful." He stepped into the room and pulled her into his arms.

"Drew." She giggled. "We were just on the plane ride here together and your room is next door. You're hugging me like you haven't seen me in ages. We've only been out of each other's sights long enough to unpack." Although she brought up the way he held her, she couldn't help but relax in his firm arms and embrace his nearness to her.

"Anytime away from you is too long." He dipped her back and tried to go in for a kiss, but he found himself tripping over the hem of her long skirt. "Renee."

"Sorry." She stepped back and bunched up her skirt at both sides. Although she had loads of material in her hands, the black skirt still managed to be well past her shins.

"Renee," he chuckled and held on to her arms, making sure she was sound on her feet after they both had almost fell, "I love you as you are, but when the length of your skirts often leaves us in hazardous situations, maybe it's time to take a few inches, yards off. Maybe even wear pants sometimes."

Renee averted eye contact with him and tried to step back, but he moved in closer to her and dropped his arms around her. "Hey, look at me." He waited until she locked eyes with him before he continued. "You don't have to change how you dress, I'll just have to be more careful when I lean in to kiss you." He smirked.

"You're right, we've almost tripped on account of my skirt lengths at least six times."

"And that's just this month," Andrew said.

Renee opened her mouth to protest, but he took the opportunity to seize her pert mouth with his.

As always, Renee kept her hands to her sides and not really giving in to the kiss, but it was apparent that Andrew was all in.

Andrew finally pulled back from her. "Renee, you know I respect you, right?"

"Yes," she murmured.

"And have I tried anything with you yet?"

"No."

"Well then, you should know that I would never try to take it there with you. I know what you're about. And like I've told you before, I love it about you. I'mma wait for you, Renee. I'll wait for our time."

"I know, it's just that—"

"It's just that what? What that creep of an ex Ted did to you?"

"Yes. He knew my views on premarital sex when he pursued me. Deceived me into thinking he was different, and then switched up on me after I was in love with him and gave in to having sex with him, unmarried. You know the rest." She lowered her head.

He lifted her chin with his fingers. "Hey, don't blame yourself for what he did to you. And we've been together all this time and I haven't tried anything with you, right?"

"Right," she said.

"You've changed me. God has changed me. Not only do I always wanna respect you, but I wanna honor God with my life, too. I'd be lying if I said I wasn't sexually attracted to you, but there's so much more to you than your looks and body. There's so much to us than lust. I love you, Renee. I'm here and I'm not going anywhere. No matter how long I have to wait. So please try not to doubt me or lump me in with the likes of that negro, Ted." He said his name through clenched teeth.

"You're right. After him and what happened between us, I made recompense by becoming a social worker and I guess I also started dressing this way to keep men's attention from me."

"Renee, dressing the way you do will never keep a man, the right man, from seeing you, the real you." He stared at her.

She blushed, even though her smooth, dark brown skin hid it.

"Come here." He pulled her into his arms again. "You okay? I mean how are you really doing? Considering last week and what you're about to do."

She relaxed her head against his solid chest and took in a deep breath. The crisp smell of his cologne always comforted her. She soon pulled back from him and walked over to her bed and sat. "I'm as good as I can be given what's going on in my life." Tears fell, although she tried to fight them. "I'm so nervous about meeting my son after all of these years. What will he say to me?" Her stomach churned as she looked up at him.

He walked over and sat next to her on the bed. He grabbed her hand to comfort her.

She looked up at him. "What if he asks why I abandoned him? Will I tell him the full truth or give him some simple answer? And as much as I appreciate you being here with me through this, I just know if my sissy were still alive, she would've insisted that she be here, comforting and nagging me through it all." She shook her head.

He gently placed his hand on her face and wiped away her tears.

"Thank you." She leaned into him for a hug, but he stole a kiss from her. His kisses drugged her and always forced her to pull away from him before he could deepen them even more so than his mere nearness to her did.

"Renee, I won't try to do more than just kiss you," he said, trying to keep her close to him, but she worked to get up from the bed.

"I believe you, Drew. I do it for me."

"What?" His head flinched back.

She averted eye contact with him and picked at her skirt. "Drew, I love you."

He thought his face would break as hard as he was smiling. Although he shared that truth with her before and often, she rarely ever said it to him. Hearing her sweet, soft voice utter the words overjoyed him.

Still not looking at him but feeling the need to say more after his bout of silence, she said, "The bible says not to give way to temptation. What I feel for you is greater than what I felt for Ted." She finally looked at him. "If I gave in to him, I'm not sure how far I'll let myself go with you. All touchy and feely, kissing any deeper than we do." She turned away from him with the end of her statement.

His smile remained wide as he stared at her long dark hair, draping over her shoulders. He had never been with her type before—sexually reserved, God-fearing—but he loved everything about her. He tapped on her shoulder until she turned back to face him with her chest caved in and her arms folded across it.

"Renee, I know how you are and why. I love it all. I keep telling you, woman, that I'll wait for you. I'm sorry if when we kiss it seems as if I try to go further with you—"

"No, you don't." She interrupted him. "I told you I worry about me."

He chuckled. "I respect you too much to let that happen between us before the designated time, even if you try to get hot in the pants with me."

She playfully hit his arms.

They both smiled.

He grabbed her hands. "If kissing you is still too much for you, I'll try to limit it to a peck on the lips every now and then. Key word, try," he said with a straight face, trying to keep from laughing.

"No, your kisses are special to me." She tried directing her vision anywhere else but him, but he held her chin and his eyes held her gaze.

"They are?" One eyebrow raised as he slowly leaned into her and placed his forehead on hers. He closed his eyes and moved in closer to her until he felt the warmth of her soft, thin lips melt against his. He squeezed her hands in his until she pulled back from him.

Her eyeballs rolled against her closed lids trying to get them to open. His kisses always seemed to take her to another place. One of tranquility and yet awareness of just how strong the love was between them. She finally forced her eyes opened and evened her breathing. "Let's get out of here."

"Okay." He smiled as she grabbed her purse and his hand in succinct movements.

***

"Renee, you know I've been to D.C. plenty of times before, you don't have to show me around." He tickled her side as they walked down the street.

She laughed, trying to escape his grasp. "Yeah, but have you seen Howard's beautiful campus before?"

"Yes," he said, hushed. He had heard the excitement in her voice back at the hotel about showing him around the campus. He avoided telling her about his many visits then, but since she'd ask him, he couldn't lie to her.

Renee raised a hesitant eyebrow at him. "When?" She had never dug into his past much, but she knew he went to school in Texas, so the thought of him having been at Howard with another woman, no matter how long ago, sent a current of jealousy flowing through her. She didn't know where the emotion had come from. She was never the jealous type, never had to be because Ted was the only other man she'd ever been with, so she wasn't familiar with competing with women for men.

She understood why women stared at Andrew as they did when they were out. No one could deny his appealing physique. Although his best friend, Kyle Irving, was a pro basketball player and he was his agent, among having other celebrity clients, his muscular body could rival that of any athlete. He had smooth, dark chocolate skin, a neatly trimmed goatee, and deep, dark inviting, yet piercing eyes. As Kim used to say that with Renee's homely looking tale on Andrew's arm, it only made sense that the stares they got begged to know how she ended up with the likes and looks of him. But he never gave her room to wonder if he had eyes for someone else. They were always locked on her.

He eyed her demeanor. "You have no reason to be jealous."

"I didn't say I was." She shrugged her shoulders and looked away.

He pulled her in closer to him and nestled his face against her ear. "I have a past that included quite a few women, across the country."

Renee tried to pull away from him, but he kept a firm grip on her waist. "But no need to worry, that man is gone. I'm a new creature." He smiled. "See, I've been studying the Word."

"I see."

They both chuckled.

"Well, since you've seen the campus, no need to see it now. But there is a little antique store I always wished I could stop in when I was here for school." She frowned. "Let's just go see if it's still there. Maybe I'll actually go in. Buy something." Dismissing her earlier thoughts, she smiled.

He hadn't missed seeing her frown, but he loved how her eyes lit up at the simplest things. And with all she was going through, he wanted her to enjoy every happy moment she could.

Their walk away from campus to the store took all of ten minutes. Andrew held the glass door open and a plastic owl stationed above the door hooted as Renee crossed the threshold.

The little store wasn't too crowded and gave the older gentleman ringing up a customer the chance to flash a quick smile at Renee and Andrew before he returned his attention to the customer in front of him.

Andrew stayed close to Renee as she ran her fingers over what looked like a hand carved jewelry case.

She looked back at him when she felt his firm grip on her waist. "You've been mighty close to me since we got in here. Are you afraid of these gently used things?"

He laughed and stepped back from her. "Afraid? Why would I be?"

She shrugged her shoulders. "I don't know. I know you can afford to buy whatever you want, no matter the cost. Maybe you think this stuff, this place, is beneath you." She dropped her gaze and went back to toying with the wooden jewelry case.

He locked his hands behind his back as he stepped closer to her. "So you pretty much think I'm shallow?"

She couldn't mistake the hurtful tone in his voice. She rushed to clarify herself. "I'm not saying that…I'm just saying…" She returned her attention to the jewelry box, unsure of what she had hinted at just moments earlier.

He chuckled and rested his forehead on the side of her face. "If you must know, me being so close to you has nothing to do with where we're at, it's because of who I'm with. I always want to be close to you."

She worked to hide her smile but it betrayed her and the corners of her mouth lifted until a wide grin spread across her face.

He took the chance to kiss her puffed cheek.

"I just wanna be near you, but hey," he stepped back from her with his hands held high as if in protest, "I'll give you your distance."

She batted her eyelashes and embraced the warm way he always made her feel. "I'm sorry if I offended you. You forgive me?"

Andrew fixed a solemn stare on her.

She held her breath unsure if things had changed between them just that quick, but when she heard the soft rumble of laughter come from him, she knew he'd been joking with her again.

"You play so much, Drew." She swatted at him, but he hopped back, avoiding her hand. She went back to investigating the trinket on the eye-level shelf when he came up behind her and snaked his arm around her again. He nestled his chin in the crook of her neck.

"I don't have a problem being in this store. In fact, I see something in the back I want to go check out." He kissed her cheek and walked off.

She smiled as she picked up a crystal angel, turning it every which way before she was forced to look over her shoulder, sensing someone was watching her. There was no one else in the shop except for the owner and Andrew engrossed in a conversation near the back. They weren't even facing her.

She shook off the odd feeling, put the angel back on the shelf, and grabbed another crystal angel next to it. It was gorgeous with its intricate carved pattern of the wings, but that eerie feeling that someone was watching her again forced her to look up and out the front window.

Her eyes blinked rapidly. "It couldn't be." She found herself mumbling as she leaned in past the figurines on the shelf to get a closer look out the window. And when she did, her head jerked back and her hand flew up to her mouth as she held her breath.

She looked back over her shoulder again to see if Andrew was near, but he wasn't. When she turned again, who she thought she had seen across the street, staring right at her, was gone.

She took deep breaths as her shaky hand put the angel back down then looked to Andrew near the back of the store. "Drew." She forced herself to speak loudly. "I think I need to go lie down for a bit before the meeting tonight."

He looked in Renee's direction. "...okay, I'll have to stop back in some other time, sir. Nice meeting you." He made it over to her and paused, noting the stunned look on her face, the visible tension in her posture. "Renee, what's wrong?" He grabbed her hand.

She looked back out the window and across the street to see only a mother leaning over a stroller, tying her toddler's shoe. "Nothing. I guess my nerves just got the best of me. I just want to go rest for a while."

"Okay." He wrapped her in his arms and kissed the top of her head before he laced his hand with hers and lead her out of the shop.

Renee held on tightly to him as they navigated the street back towards her hotel.

Had she been mistaken and her mind was playing tricks on her, or was it really *him* she'd seen?

3

Pam

Vance stepped in the foyer of his home and dropped his messenger bag on the floor just under where he would soon hang his coat. It was six in the evening and he knew from a brief text conversation with Pam earlier that she was at home.

He sighed as he hung his coat, and then drudged slow steps to the stairs that would lead him to the sunken living room he knew he was sure to find his wife.

He didn't smell any evidence of food being ready for him to devour, but that didn't matter. His nerves were too frayed to eat. He didn't know how Pam would take the news he had to share with her. It was something he had been working towards, dreaming of, but given her close ties with the sisterhood and it being so soon after Kim's passing, he knew it may not have been the best time to broach the subject.

"Hey, babe," he said as he drew closer to her.

Her voice was faint as she offered him a hushed response.

Tears streamed her face and her chest rose and fell rapidly as she laid curled up on the oversized chair near the fireplace.

Vance wasn't sure if her cries were due to the novel she had in her hand or from recently losing one of her best friends, but he'd find out soon as he took his shoes off, loosened his tie, and positioned himself in the chair to pull her into his arms. He pulled the book from her hand and dropped it on the floor near the chair.

Accepting his embrace, she wrapped her arms around his waist and let her head rest on his chest.

"You okay?" He kissed the top of her head.

She shook her head and sniffled.

He rubbed her back trying to soothe her. "I know how connected you can get to the characters in the book. Is it the characters or about Kim?"

"Kim," she whimpered.

"You wanna talk about it?"

She lifted off him and rolled over so that she still laid on his chest but could look at him.

He hated seeing how pitiful she looked, and while maybe his thoughts shouldn't have gone there, he couldn't help himself, she was his wife. He always craved intimacy with her. He leaned down and pressed his lips to hers, commencing a slow and endearing kiss between them.

When their lips parted, he stared into her glistening eyes and then swiped the tears falling on her face. "I love you."

"I love you, too. And I miss her so much," she said and broke eye contact with him. She laid her head on his chest again.

He wrapped his arms tighter around her and rested his chin on the top of her head.

"This is not right. She should still be alive. We all should be in D.C. with Renee. Supporting her in meeting her son."

"But she didn't want you all there with her, babe."

She hiccupped, trying to talk through her sobs. "I know, but if Kim would've been here, that wouldn't have mattered. Kim would've bulldozed her way there and happily dragged me and Monica along with her."

"True." He held a faint smile remembering Kim, his feisty employee and who'd also become a friend, an inherited sister because of his relationship with Pam.

She looked up at him through blurry vision. "You know, Renee has always been the most naive and the fragile out of the four of us. I don't doubt that Andrew doesn't love her and can be there for her. But it should be me and Monica there with her. The three of us have to band together more now than ever." She squeezed him tighter.

Although she barely made a sound, the fast rise and fall of her chest against him and the knowledge that his shirt was soaked where her head laid, let him know that she had given herself over to simply crying. Her trembling body clued him in that she might not stop anytime soon.

He took a deep breath and settled more into the chair. He held her tighter and rubbed her back in big and what he hoped was soothing circles.

His evening wasn't panning out the way he'd hoped. Given Pam's sister-like bond to Kim and it being so close to her passing, he knew he'd still have to comfort his wife, but after the great news he had received at work, he wished he could've shared it with his her the minute he got home. But the timing was all wrong.

As the principal, he'd turned one of the city's worst, low-performing elementary schools, riddled with misbehaved students, into the high achieving academic center it had become. He and the staff had worked tirelessly to redirect the kids' behavior because he felt they deserved a safe and well-functioning place of learning. And while all he ever wanted to do was to change the lives of his students, it didn't hurt that his efforts had yielded him recognition beyond his wildest dreams.

He had been interviewed by several news outlets on the changes he had made at the school and in the community. Yeah, he'd heard talks of the Board of Education of Chicago wanting to move him around the city to replicate what he'd done at Jensen. He was up for that challenge, but never had he thought that Memphis's school board would call and offer him a position. One in which he would spearhead a division to intensively train principals and staffs there to transform their schools as he had Jensen.

In Memphis, he would be the principal of all principals. How could he not be excited to make that kind of change there?

However, looking down at his sobbing wife and pulling her even closer, he knew he couldn't share the news with her just yet. Taking the job would mean they'd have to move to Memphis. Away from Chicago. Away from what was left of the sisterhood.

No, he'd save that conversation for another day. Instead, he gathered Pam up in his arms and held her close to him as he went to lay her down in their bed.

4

Monica

"Come here, baby," Monica said, squeezing Kalia tightly and blowing kisses on her cheek. The sound of her daughter's laughter warmed her heart and gave her cries a reprieve, considering she'd just buried her best friend the week before. "I just love you so much," she said, tickling her daughter, squirming and laughing in her arms.

She repositioned Kalia to face her son and said in a baby voice, "Wook at your bruhda. He's sleeping, why won't you go to sleep?"

Kalia turned to face her mother and wrapped her arms around her neck.

"I love you too, baby."

Just then, the alarm sounded and Monica knew that Keith was home.

She placed Kalia on her mat filled with toys. "Mommy's gonna go say hi to Daddy."

Kalia was lost in playing with the glowing worm and didn't bother to look up at her mother.

Monica lifted up from the couch and rushed to the front door to catch Keith before he disappeared in the house as he had been doing when coming home from work since the funeral.

"Babe, how was your day?" she said, smiling as she held her arms open to embrace him.

Before Kim's death, Keith wouldn't have wasted any time in wrapping his arms around her and kissing her in a desirous way that confirmed his love for her. But with his shoulders slumped and his arms down to his side, not returning her embrace, she knew something was off with him.

He soon pulled away from her, carrying his suitcase with him.

"Keith, wait, we need to talk," she said to his back as he walked towards his home office.

He didn't respond. She looked back at her daughter, grateful that she had finally fell asleep on the floor. She would try to hurry and talk to Keith before she had to get back and check on the twins.

She looked back to the direction in which he walked and took a deep breath. Not to say that everything had been perfect in their relationship, especially considering what it took for them to get together after years of secretly loving each other and neither making a move, but their relationship, their marriage never involved helping the other to cope with the death of a close loved one.

She didn't know exactly how to broach the subject with Keith. She had been letting him grieve in his own way, but that day had to be the last day of that. He had to know he could depend on her and she could depend on him to stay open to her. She was grieving, too. They needed each other to get past this stage of grief.

She finally made it to the slightly ajar door of his office and peeked in. His head was in his hands, but when she fully opened the door, he sat up and directed his attention to the paperwork spread out on his desk.

"Keith," she said, stepping into the room and making her way to stand next to him. She perched her butt on his desk.

"It's late, you've been at work all day. Won't you just come and spend some time with me and the kids?" She reached to touch his hand and felt him stiffen.

That stung. She took a deep breath and slowly pulled her hand back.

"I have work to do," he said in a clipped tone.

"I know how ambitious you are at work, but before…" She let her words trail off, not wanting to directly mention Kim's death. "But before last week, when you came home, you were present. You spent time with the twins and then time with me."

"I have a lot going on at work that has to be taken care of."

"You went back to work Monday, right after— I'm certain you can get time off to grieve. I think you need it."

"I don't need anything but for you to let me get back to this project I'm working on," he said without looking up at her.

Monica stood up and cleared her throat. She was trying to keep a cool head, keep her tears from falling. He had never been so cold to her.

"You leave early in the morning, you come home late. You don't even greet me or the kids. We miss you. Talk to me, please. I know you're hurting, but now is not the time to pull away from me. We're supposed to get through this together. I loved her just as much as you did."

Nostrils flaring, chest heaving, Keith stood up and peered down at his wife. "Loved her? I still love her. She was my sister, my triplet. She was here last week and gone now. How am I supposed to get over that?"

Monica reached up to caress his face. "I still love her, too, baby. We always will."

He inhaled a deep breath and then stepped back from her.

"Keith, don't pull away from me."

"I'm not," he said dismissively as he took his seat again at his desk.

"You can't keep ignore dealing with Kim's loss if that's what you're trying to do."

He pounded his fist on the desk, and then let his head fall into his hands.

"We can get through this together, baby. Don't shut me out." She leaned over, resting her chin on his head and rubbed his back.

Keith sat still, silent for a moment before he said, "Monica...I have to get out of here." He stood.

"Where are you going?" She grabbed his wrist, stopping him from leaving his office.

"I just have to go." He never looked back at her.

Tears watered her face quickly, but she took deep breaths to calm herself. She was pregnant and didn't want to add any more stress to the baby than the last few weeks already had.

Never before had Keith talked to her the way he did, been so cold to her the way he had. Since they had been together, she didn't know what it was like for him to not stare at her with tenderness, grab her in his arms, and whisper sweet nothings to her. But this cold Keith she'd encountered the past week, she needed him to go away as soon as possible and return her loving husband back to her.

She couldn't help but sob softly as she walked back into the living room and grabbed her kids one by one to ready them for bed.

She understood he needed to grieve his own way, but shutting her out was not the best way. She just hoped that their marriage, her heart, could survive his mourning.

5

Renee

Renee's jean skirt covered knees knocked against Andrew's as they sat at a linen-covered table in the hotel's restaurant. She could barely contain her jitters as they waited for her son, Isaiah's, adoptive parents, the Browns, to arrive.

"Renee, sweetie, it's going to be okay." He clutched her hand and pulled it up to his lips, pecking a sweet kiss to the back of it.

She looked in his direction and offered him a faint, brief smile before focusing her attention back to the open entryway of the restaurant. She wanted to spot them the minute they arrived. She had face-timed the Browns, so she knew how they looked.

"Renee, trust me. Everything will be fine." This time, Andrew pulled her into him with his arm wrapped around her shoulder and pecked kisses to her forehead.

Relishing in the comfort he provided her, she let her eyelids close and took a deep, calming breath, silently thanking God that Andrew was in her life and that he was there for her. "Thank you," she said, opening her eyes.

The smile lifting the corners of her mouth morphed her facial features into a slacked jaw and wide eyes as she focused on the Browns being escorted to her table.

Andrew squeezed her hand before bracing it on her elbow to help her stand to welcome them to the table. "Hello." He reached forward and shook Mr. Brown's hand then Mrs. Brown's hand. "I'm Andrew, Renee's boyfriend."

"Good to meet you. Renee shared you'd be coming with her when we talked this past week." Mrs. Brown smiled.

Andrew looked over to see Renee still stunned and speechless. "Renee."

"Hi," she said low as she warily shook the Browns' proffered hands.

"Please, have a seat." Andrew extended his hand for the couple to sit in the two empty seats across from him and Renee.

"Thank you." Mr. Brown helped his wife to be seated before taking his.

Andrew followed suit, helping a stalled Renee sit.

A waiter came up to the table. "May I start you all off with drinks?"

"We're fine with the water you brought us earlier, but Mr. and Mrs. Brown, what would you all like to drink?" Andrew said.

"Two waters with lemons and lite ice would be just fine." Mrs. Brown spoke for herself and her husband.

"Coming right up." The waiter walked off.

The Browns stared at Renee as politely as they could.

"She's a bit nervous," Andrew said and then leaned in to whisper to Renee. "Babe, it's okay, just be you."

She looked at him, smiled, and redirected her attention to the Browns. "Mr. and Mrs. Brown—"

"Please call us Kristen and Josh," Mrs. Brown implored.

"Okay." Renee smiled. "We talked about quite a bit this past week, but there are some details I omitted."

Josh squeezed his wife's hand knowing the clearing of her throat meant she was preparing herself for the information that was about to be shared. He knew she always did that whenever someone may be attempting to throw her off guard.

Renee noted the tension on Kristen's face. "I'm sorry, I didn't mean that to sound like I live a rough life, one riddled with drugs or something and that's why I gave him up. I told you all I was young and not ready for the responsibility of raising a child, but the truth of the matter is I was in an abusive relationship when I conceived, my son, Isaiah…" Renee's voice trailed off. It seemed odd to her to say that he was her son and yet they were the ones who had raised him. But it was the truth nonetheless. She had carried him and had given birth to him.

"The abuse was so bad that I couldn't stand to let him be around his father, not to mention he pretty much made me give him up for adoption."

"We're sorry to hear that," Josh said.

"So, you see, it's not that I didn't love my son and that I haven't thought about him every day of his life, I have. The guilt of giving him up weighed me down for so long. Being a social worker, I know the good and bad effects that adoption can have on the child adopted. I know the questions they ask themselves growing up about their birth parents." She squeezed Andrew's strong hand more so for his benefit than for the comfort he had been providing her.

Just then, the waiter returned and placed their glasses in front of each of them. "Are you all ready to order?"

Andrew took the initiative to speak up for everyone knowing that Renee wasn't done with the speech she had been rehearsing. He didn't want the act of ordering food make her lose the confidence she'd built up to face the couple. "Can you give us just a few more minutes?"

"Yes, sir." The waiter nodded and walked off again.

"Sorry if you all are hungry and wanted to place your orders but I know Renee needs to get this all off her chest."

"It's fine. We can wait to order," Kristen said, "please continue, Renee." She offered a sincere smile to Renee.

"Like I was saying, my wanting to meet him didn't come out of the blue, it's always been there. I was just too afraid to do something about it. The loss I experienced from my sister's death jolted me into wanting to seize the moments I have left in life. I love Isaiah and I want him to know that. I want him to be able to ask me anything he may have been wanting to know during these years of his life. And please know that I'm grateful for you opening up to me this week, agreeing to meet me here today, and most importantly allowing me in my son's life. You'll never know how much all of this means to me." Renee's eyes glossed over with unshed tears. Soon, tears tracked her face.

Kristen handed her a napkin and patted her free hand across the table. "Just breathe."

Renee took a deep breath.

"Given that it wasn't a closed adoption, we knew this day was a possibility." Kristen took a deep breath. "Honestly, although it may seem selfish on our part, we kind of hoped this day would never come."

"I can understand that. I've seen it so many times, but I also know, when done right, it's a healthy part of the child's growing process." Renee pursed her lips, not rearing for a fight, but not knowing what to make of the fretful look on Josh's face as he shifted in his seat.

He looked to her with sympathy in his eyes. "Renee, we understand your desire to be in his life and we really do sympathize with you. Isaiah's known for a long time that he was adopted. He's always said that didn't matter because we were his real parents in every sense that mattered."

Tears slowly trailed Renee's face again. Josh's last statement pained her and she didn't know where he was going with his speech. Although he tried to keep his voice even, there was still a defense to it.

"Josh is right. You know that since we broke the news to Isaiah last week about you coming into town to meet him, he's avoided face time with you."

Renee's shoulders slumped recalling the conversation the night Kristen called her back to let her know that Isaiah declined face time with her as a means to break the ice.

"As the week went on of talking to you, you shared that you'd already brought your plane ticket here for this weekend. Again, we sympathize with you and thought perhaps we could convince him to give you a chance, at least meet you. We were leery about telling you not to come because he may have changed his mind last minute, but unfortunately, Renee, he's standing his ground in not wanting to meet you." She reached over and patted Renee's trembling hand, rattling the silverware spread out on a napkin to the right of her.

Andrew squeezed her hand.

"We're sorry that you came all of this way for nothing. We're sorry that we couldn't make things happen more in your favor, but we have to keep his best interest in mind. We won't force him to do something he's not ready to do." She looked at a shaky Renee and then at her husband. "Maybe we should just leave now."

Josh stood and then pulled his wife's chair back to help her up from her seat.

Renee dropped her head in her open palms and cried as Andrew stood and shook the Browns' hands before they left the table.

"Come on, let's get you out of here." Andrew gathered Renee's trembling body up from her seat and held her close as he guided her to the elevators and up to her room.

6

Darius

A series of grunts came from under a pillow in the darkened living room.

Darius grabbed the pillow from his face, threw it to the floor, and then rolled over on his back on the couch, rubbing his eyes. He slowly opened them, trying to adjust to the darkness his house hosted. It was as dark as he felt on the inside.

It had been Kim who had brightened the dimly lit area of his love life, but now, she was gone and the pain of that knowledge kept him hidden in his apartment since her funeral.

He could only imagine how many missed calls were in his call log, but he couldn't check it even if he cared to. He was certain his phone had powered off since he hadn't charged it all week. He didn't even know where it was.

The only reason he was moving from the couch at that point was because his body alerted him that he had to use the bathroom.

He spun until his one-sock-on-one-sock-off feet hit his hardwood floors.

He rubbed his eyes one last time with the palm of his hands before he stood up and let out a loud string of expletives as he stretched his stiff, broad back.

His gray jogging pants hung low on his trim waist as he made his way down the hall and to the bathroom.

Opening the door, he winced at the light from the window flooding the space. He handled his business, washed his hands, and hurried up closing the door behind him to return his house to perfect darkness.

All he wanted to do was get back to the couch and let unconsciousness take him over until his body required another bathroom break, but his parched throat directed his feet to the kitchen.

As if on cue, his stomach rumbled loudly the minute his hand touched the refrigerator handle.

"Shut up," he said to his stomach as he reached past containers of what he knew had to be spoiled food in them. He grabbed a bottle of water and before closing the door.

He'd continue to ignore his hunger for two good reasons. One being, he didn't have anything worth eating and two, he didn't care to eat.

He gulped the water down in no time and then worked his way back to the living room to go back to sleep, but not before staring at the bright digits on his microwave.

He had one of those sophisticated models where it not only shared the time, but also the calendar date. Eyebrows furrowed, he stared at it realizing what the day meant. It was Friday and if he wanted to actually be a part of the comedy tour he'd agreed to in a fleeting moment of contentment around Kim's death, he'd have to get it together and quick to make the first show the next night.

He cursed out loud hating that he'd agreed to it. If he wanted to remain a man of his word, he'd have to get on the flight in the morning.

Bypassing his front door and ignoring the sudden banging on it, he went over to the base of his couch and ruffled through the throw pillows strewn on the floor until he found his phone. He tapped the screen to no avail, confirming his phone was dead and would need to be charged.

He stalked to his bedroom in search of his phone charger when the sound of his front door ready to come off its hinges forced him back into his living room.

He rushed in to see that his door was still locked in spite of the hard beating it was receiving. His shoulders bounced in tandem with the sarcastic chuckle he let out as he walked back over to the couch and flopped down. He plugged his charger into an extension cord nearby and then plugged it into his phone.

He wasn't alarmed by the constant banging on the door because judging from the deep voices and name calling coming from the other side of the door, he knew it was only his best of friends, Anthony Parham and brothers, Marcus and Vance Sutherland trying to get in.

"Darius, open this door before we bust it down like we've done before," Vance said, pressed against the door.

"We know you're in there and we know you can hear us," Anthony added.

Darius didn't bother to respond knowing he'd indeed locked the deadbolt seeing as though at least one of the guys had a key to get into his house in case of an emergency. But emergencies hadn't been the only times they used their keys; they used it once when they had bulldozed their way in to convince him to go to Kim's funeral.

"D, man, just let us in. We just wanna see that you're okay. We swear we won't stay long," Marcus said.

Darius growled and covered his face with his hands as his head fell back. He just wished they would leave him alone. But hadn't he done the same when he chased after Vance when he and Marcus found out their father had been killed back when they were in undergrad?

Knowing how supportive of each other they were nagged at him and forced him off the couch to unlock the door and let his pesky friends in.

He regretted opening the door immediately when the hallway lights streamed in his place.

"Should've known it would be dark in here," Vance said as he patted Darius on the back and walked past him.

"You good, bro?" Anthony asked, the last one to walk into the apartment. He went in search of a seat to occupy before focusing his attention back on Darius.

Darius returned to his seat, and by that time, his phone had enough charge to power up.

When on, he began scrolling through his text log in search of the tour managers thread. As he suspected, he'd missed several texts and reading through some of them, the manager informed him he'd missed several of his calls as well. He said he knew he was dealing with the death of a loved one and would assume he was still set to start the tour with them. He went on to say that the only way he'd know if he needed to back out was if he called him personally.

"So, you're just gonna sit there and ignore us?" Anthony asked, notably the most uncouth of the quartet of friends.

Darius finally looked up from his phone. "You come to my house, uninvited, bogart your way in here *and* demand I give you my undivided attention?"

"I see you're not too far from your old self." Vance chuckled.

"My phone's been off all week."

"We know," the guys concerted.

"Whatever. Not interested in responding to anyone but the tour manager, Greg."

"We're just checking on you bro. We know how you are and we've tried to give you your space this past week to deal in your own way, but we couldn't let another day go by without checking up on you," Marcus said.

Darius grunted.

"We can see you aren't doing all that good." Vance chuckled. "Wrinkled clothes, looks like you lost a little weight, and that scruffy facial hair isn't for you, bro. Anthony, you'll have to hook him up soon. Like ASAP."

"I'm ready whenever you are, D. Especially if you're going on that tour starting tomorrow." Anthony raised a brow.

"I don't want to talk about that now, so don't ask." Darius gruffed.

"Okay, so given that you've just turned your phone back on, I take it you actually haven't talked to Mrs. Williams?" Vance asked.

"No. Why would I?" Darius's eyebrows knitted together.

"Because, she's been trying to reach out to you all week," Vance said.

Darius sat up and to the end of the couch. "Know why?"

"Pam said she wants to keep in touch with you," Vance said.

Darius rubbed his face slowly before looking back at Vance.

"Don't look at me like that. I didn't put the thought in her head. But I will tell you that Pam told me Mrs. Williams said that seeing as though you were the last man, the only man that she knew her daughter ever loved, you're worth knowing. Call her."

What Vance had just shared with him was heavy. Not only did he need to make the decision as to whether or not to actually go on the tour but now whether or not he would indeed forge a relationship with Mrs. Williams.

He was still contemplating the first, but the latter, he'd at least give it a try. And although it might've made more sense to distance himself as far away from possible from anyone that reminded him of Kim and what he'd never have with her, he oddly felt he owed it to Kim, to himself, to at least call Mrs. Williams.

He scrolled through his voicemails that had been converted to text and found her number. He pressed the green button and held the phone up to his ear until he heard her say hello.

"Hello, Mrs. Williams, this is Darius."

7

Pam

A month had gone by since Kim passed and Pam was finally able to not breakdown at work. It was awfully strange not seeing her best friend in the building anymore, but day by day she was getting stronger with handling Kim's absence.

It didn't help that Renee hadn't returned from D.C. yet; that troubled her. However, she took a little comfort in knowing that she talked to her daily and prayed to God that He would keep her and bless her outcome with her son.

The school day had ended and she was more than ready to go home and relax her mind, prepare dinner before Vance came home, and then spend some quality time with her husband.

With her laptop bag and tote bag full of papers she was supposed to grade that night but probably wouldn't, she made her way into the main office to clock out.

It wasn't that late so she didn't understand where the majority of the office staff had slipped off to. Only the office clerk, Shelly, was there and busy typing away on her computer. Shelly looked up briefly and mouthed good night to Pam before returning her attention to the computer screen.

Pam clocked out and rounded the desk to check her mailbox one last time before heading out.

She headed towards the door that would put her closer to the stairwell that led to the staff parking lot. Her hand had barely touched the doorknob when she clearly heard Mr. Hubert, the COO of their network of schools, telling Vance, just behind his office door, "We hate to see you leave us, given what you've done with this fine school, but we're all for ambition, and I know you'll be great in your new position in Memphis."

Her breath hitched. Her ears perked up. Had she heard him correctly? *Position in Memphis?*

Not one to eavesdrop, but taken back by the admission she'd just heard, her feet wouldn't move. Vance hadn't responded yet and she just couldn't move until he said something. Hopefully, something to dismiss Mr. Hubert's claim, but she needed to hear him say something. Maybe then her heartbeat would return to some type of normalcy.

"Mr. Hubert, I, I, I—"

"I would be speechless too if I were offered that kind of position, but I know you'll be great in it. Pretty much running your own district."

Pam's already voluptuous chest puffed up and filled with air just waiting for Vance to dispute Mr. Hubert, but the only thing she heard was, "You're right, being offered the position is an honor. I can't wait to get started." She didn't miss the hesitancy in his voice with the last of his words.

She finally released her breath, but a myriad of emotions filled her. She was mad at him for not telling her about the offer since it seemed like this wasn't his first-time hearing of it. On the other hand, she couldn't help but to be happy for him. Running his own school district and duplicating the success he had at their school had been a personal and professional desire of his for so long.

She knew she shouldn't have been eavesdropping, but it was too late to do anything about that, but what she couldn't do was wait until he got home that night. She'd give him a second to see if he'd come clean with her, if not she'd just have to be the one to confront him about what she heard. Him accepting the job would mean her moving away from the remainder of the sisterhood and that wasn't something she was sure she could do.

8

Monica

"Thank you so much, Mom and Dad, for watching them while I go to the doctor. It'd be too much trying to manage them there," Monica said as she took Kalia's coat off the wiggling toddler.

"Watch them?" Mrs. Williams said with a raised eyebrow. "I don't consider it watching them, shoot, I'm spending time with my grandchildren. Quality time. I love them so much. Especially that little Kalia who looks and is starting to act like her Auntie Kim." She cleared her throat, staring at Kalia's little pie shaped face and bright, round, doe eyes. Mrs. Williams' eyes glossed over. She had to redirect the conversation and her attention. "So, will Keith meet you at the doctor?"

Monica hadn't told anyone how distant Keith had been with her the past month. She definitely wasn't going to share it with his mother. She saw the way she was looking at Kalia and she could tell she was trying not to get choked up about her granddaughter looking just like her recently deceased daughter, so she saw no good reason to bring up the fact that her son wasn't acting right where she was concerned. She'd just continue to deal with it on her own, in prayer and in patience. "Only if he can reschedule his meeting." Monica feigned indifference.

Better yet, she flat out lied to Mrs. Williams. Keith was the boss of his division in the company and could work from home as often as he needed to and reschedule meetings as desired. He'd done it all the time with her first pregnancy. But now he didn't hesitate to tell her that work was keeping him from being home and present with her and their kids for the minimal amount of time he was there, which was pretty much sleeping hours.

"Keith miss a doctor's appointment? He never missed one when you were pregnant with these two," Mrs. Williams said, putting Keith Jr. in his high chair so that she could feed them their noon snacks.

"Like I said, Momma Williams, he'll be there if he can reschedule his meeting. Speaking of, let me get out of here before I end up late and having to reschedule this visit."

"Alright, Mon, see you later," Mrs. Williams said as Monica walked up to her and gave her a quick hug before kissing the twins and rushing out of the door.

She wouldn't even bother calling Keith to see if he would indeed show up. It'd probably go straight to his voicemail, or if she called the office, his assistant would more than likely say he was unavailable at the time as had been the responses to her outreach to him all morning long.

***

"Okay, Monica, you sure you don't want to wait until your husband gets here?" Dr. Franklin asked as she adjusted the sonogram screen so that Monica would be able to see it.

"No, he won't be coming." Monica cleared her throat and adjusted a little on the exam table.

"Oh," she said with a slight hesitation. "Well, we've already checked your weight which is where it should be given your height and that you're a little under three months. Your blood pressure is just fine, too, so let's just check the baby's heartbeat and growth. And remember, this will be cold." She rubbed the jelly on Monica's firm, but rounding stomach.

Seeing as though she was extremely ticklish, Monica yelped louder than perhaps any other pregnant woman would during the exam.

Dr. Franklin chuckled. "The twins got to be super ticklish from you."

"Yes, they did." Monica smiled. "They giggle so loud and so long when touched, but I love the sound of it."

Dr. Franklin picked up the wand. "Okay, I'm going to rub this across your belly. We should hear a strong heartbeat and see it reading across the screen up top and you know we'll see your little one."

"Yes." Her heartbeat sped up noting the surprised look on Dr. Franklin's face. "What is it?" She tried to sit up and look at the monitor at the same time.

"Oh, it's nothing bad, depending on your wishes right now, but if you look at the screen here and here," she pointed to two separate locations, "you'll see that those are two separate sacs, like before, with the twins."

Hunched back on her elbows and head cocked to the side, Monica stared absentmindedly at Dr. Franklin. "So you're telling me that I'm pregnant with twins? Again?"

"Yes," Dr. Franklin said, smiling.

Monica fell back on the exam table, overcome with emotions as her eyes filled with tears and then spilled down her face.

"You okay?"

"I just need a second."

"Okay. Just let me clean the gel off your belly and I'll step out for a second." Dr. Franklin made quick work of removing the gel, tidying up, and then softly closing the door behind her.

The minute the door closed, Monica allowed herself to cry without restraint.

It was a given that she was happy that she could even be pregnant seeing as though for so many years she thought she could never conceive due to what her doctors had said were post-complications from an abortion she had when she was in college. Having the twins, taking care of them, watching them grow, and now pregnant with another set of twins, filled her heart with more joy than she could ever articulate. But all of that glee bubbling inside of her was overshadowed by the fact that she was at the doctor alone, without her husband, finding out such news.

The past month had been pretty hard on her, functioning almost like a single parent while taking care of the kids, grieving the loss of her best friend, and still running her event company. She had been delegating responsibility of the events she was booked for to her staff, but she did want to get back to what she loved to do, soon, if at least for a while. She wouldn't dare be responsible for yet another two lives to care for without the help of her husband. She understood he was grieving, but now more than ever was the time for him to do better by her and their kids.

Being alone in the doctor's office, learning that they'd be having twins again, recounting how long it'd been since Keith had looked at her lovingly, last kissed her, held her in his arms, how distant he'd been from her, it all made her break down crying.

9

Renee

"Maybe I should just go back home and forget about trying to connect with him…but I don't want him to think that I don't care and would give up so easily on him again. Maybe that's what he really thinks and that's why he doesn't even wanna bother seeing me." Renee wiped away a tear.

"Renee, breathe," Andrew said through the phone as he sat in a conference room in L.A.

"I am."

"No, really take a breath. I see I need to come back there with you. I have a meeting in twenty minutes and then one at nine a.m. tomorrow, but I can get on a plane right after and can probably be in D.C. by around six at the latest."

"That won't be necessary, Drew."

"No, I want to see you. It's been a week, way too long as far as I'm concerned. Plus, you need someone there to keep you calm. It'll be just as beneficial for me as it will be for you." He smiled.

"I miss you, too, Drew, but please, stay there and do what you need to do. Besides, didn't you say that you had a meeting in Seattle in a couple of days?"

"Yeah, but I can reschedule it or do a video conference. You're most important to me."

"Drew, really, I'm fine. I think I'll go home tomorrow anyway. Regroup and give my bank account a break from paying this hotel bill." She chuckled, trying to lighten up her somber mood.

"I told you I'd take care of that for you."

"No, you don't have to."

"Renee, I know this is important to you. I know you don't like taking things from me, me buying you stuff, but you're just gonna have to get used to me doing for you."

She smiled wide, although she knew he couldn't see it. She had been fighting him showering gifts on her. The time they spent together, the way he looked at her, held her in his arms was more valuable than anything he could ever buy her. His love for her was apparent and priceless.

"Okay."

"Good. So now you can stay there as long as you want to. Matter of fact, I'll call the front desk and square everything away before I head into my meeting."

"Drew, thanks…I love you."

Hearing her sound out her feelings for him so soon since the last time she said it, made his chest swell with pride, a joy he hadn't felt in a long time, a feeling he would never tire of. He knew she didn't say she loved him that particular time because he would be paying for her hotel stay, but because she was actively letting her guard down. He knew she was letting him fill the space in her heart she thought would never be occupied again by a man after what she went through with Ted. "I love you, too, baby."

She giggled. The way he called her baby warmed her insides. "I'll call you after I meet with the Browns."

"Okay, but are you sure you don't want me to be there with you? I can fix my schedule and try to get there today."

"No, Drew. I'm fine meeting with them again by myself. Have a great day."

"You, too."

They hung up the phone and Renee dressed in layers to explore D.C. before her meeting later.

She had spoken on the phone with the Browns often, sharing more about herself, hoping that they could somehow convince her son to give her a chance, meet her face to face, but each time, they came back with the same report—Isaiah didn't want to meet her.

Each no pricked her heart, but since it had already been shattered by Kim's death and never having her son in her life, she felt the only way she'd be able to mend it is if she reconciled with him. She wouldn't ever give up on trying to be in his life.

She was grateful for her layers as the chilly temperature hovered around her once she stepped outside of the hotel.

Under the tight watch of Ted in undergrad, she didn't venture out into D.C. back then. Being there now with nothing to do but bid her time until she met her son, she'd been visiting all of the historical monuments, sites, and museums that the city had to offer. Thankfully, she'd bought her tickets online so she wouldn't have to wait outside in the long line to enter the National Black Museum.

Another benefit of getting her ticket online and not having to wait in line was that she hoped she could avoid that feeling of being followed, as she had been feeling many of the days she explored the city. It was that same creepy feeling she got when she and Andrew were at the antique shop and she thought she saw *him* standing across the street.

Each time she was out, the hairs on her arms seemed to raise, her breathing stalled, and she warily scanned a room trying to see who gave her the uneasy feeling. She never saw *him* or anyone who looked to be spying on her, let alone paying attention to her. She soon dismissed her thoughts and immersed herself again in whatever exhibit she had gone to see.

She stepped into the welcoming area of the museum and not knowing exactly where to go, smiled and guided her steps to the information desk to grab a brochure. She needed to see where her exploration of the museum would take her first in the building.

Never much into music and fashion, she decided she'd save those sections for last in her visit and instead got on the elevator and went straight down to C2, the level that allowed her to sit at a mock lunch counter. Once there, she went between looking at the screens on the wall past the counter detailing certain events from the student led sit-ins at restaurants back in the 1960s to following through the links on the interactive screen on the countertop.

She was knowledgeable about much of the civil rights movement, but a weight still overtook her learning even more about the sit-ins. Being asked some of the questions and scenarios that many of the students had to ask themselves made her embrace just how headstrong and determined they were to bring about change back then.

It was late afternoon during the week, so it wasn't too crowded, save the tourists and a few groups of high school aged students' chatter softly around her.

She looked back at the screen on the countertop and weighed the answer to the question she was being asked when the eerie feeling she had been experiencing since she'd been in D.C. crept back on her. Her nerves rattled in the pit of her stomach. She took a deep breath and slowly lifted her head to look to the left and right of her.

Satisfied that no one was looking in her direction, she returned her attention back to the screen.

A few moments passed and someone bumped into her as a group of students walked past. It wasn't a normal, mistaken bump because the person had seemed to intentionally graze her arm. The act made her back erect straight and snap her neck in the direction the kids were traveling.

None of them looked a day over sixteen nor did any of them look back at her. *I'm tripping.* She once again looked back at the screen since she had one more slide to complete before her time at the counter would end.

She gave her last answer and stood. She had been sitting there for a while so she stretched high and wide as she thanked God that she didn't grow up in that time and have to endure what they did, yet grateful that they fought some battles that she would never have to. She knew their actions paved a smoother way for her. For that, she would be eternally grateful.

Having looked at the brochure long and hard to know exactly what exhibits she wanted to see during that day's visit, she knew the one she dreaded visiting was there and had decided not to see it. At fourteen, he was about the same age as Isaiah when it happened to him and stalled her from wanting to witness it, but there was a magnetic-like pull of her in its direction.

Being so close to it, she made her way to take in the museums retelling of the story of Emmett Till. She walked past an in-wall glass display of newspaper clippings of the ordeal and immediately turned her head away from it when one newspaper cover honored the mother's wishes and decided to show his face as was, after the beating.

She took a deep breath after she crossed the threshold and followed the path leading to his casket. The soul stirring voice of Mahalia Jackson singing *Amazing Grace* rumbled through the speakers as she was given the opportunity to view the casket he once laid in along with the clothes he wore at the funeral. The picture of his maimed face was fixed at the top of the open, but glass covered casket.

She sniffled and quickly wiped away a tear. She pulled herself away from the images and text surrounding the casket only to be drawn into another small room, still apart of the exhibit, where a video retold the tale surrounding Emmet Till's death.

She needed to occupy her time until she would meet up with Kristen again, but maybe the National Black Museum wasn't the best choice for her. Everything she'd seen up that point had her somber, not to mention the eerie feeling of being watched had crept back up on her.

She thought she was the only one in the exhibit at the time, but she quickly leaned back into the other room checking to see if someone was indeed there, staring at her.

She didn't see anyone, so she straightened her body. Just then, she heard what sounded like a jacket brush against the wall on the opposite side of the partition she stood next to.

Although she led the investigative team of social workers, she was never one to investigate where odd sounds came from when she was alone. She picked up a fast pace and fled the room with a quickness probably not permitted in the museum.

Once outside of the exhibit and back amongst a healthy-sized crowd, she exhaled a deep breath she hadn't even registered she was holding. She looked down at her watch to see that she had a few more hours left before she needed to head over to the restaurant. *Might as well stay and take advantage of the rest of my time here.*

She continued through as much of the museum as she could with the time she had left. There was so much to see, contemplate. She would've truly enjoyed herself had she not been so busy looking over her shoulders sensing that someone was following her. *How could it be him? Is he out of jail?*

***

"Hello, I'd like a booth, please. Preferably one all the way in the back. No one able to be behind me," Renee said.

The waiter paused to examine her with a calculated scan of his eyes, then said, "Let me go check if any of our corner booths are available. I'll be right back." He offered her a strained smile and walked off.

She had been trying to shake off the feeling that she was being followed all the way to the restaurant. Sitting in a corner booth would give her some type of reassurance, but the look on the approaching waiter's face didn't seem favorable.

"Sorry ma'am, I have side booths available close to the back, but it's not the last one as you requested. Would you still like a booth?"

"Sure," she said and nodded. "He has not given me the spirit of fear but of power, love, and of a sound mind," she mumbled.

"You talking to me?" he asked with a raised brow, looking back at her.

"No."

"Okay, follow me then."

As she followed him, she thought about peeking into the booth behind where he was sitting her to see who was seated but she knew the gesture would be strange. What would she say if those seated questioned why she was all up in their faces? "He has not given me the spirit of fear," she softly repeated to herself as she took her seat in the booth. *Maybe I should've asked Drew to come back with me. Or better yet, as crazy as she could be at times and would probably act, my sissy should be here with me.* She took a deep breath trying to breathe through not crying but found herself laughing at the new thought that she had just come across. *I bet if she were still alive, she would've gone over to that house by now and snatched Isaiah up by his collar and told him that he better give me a chance. That he'd learn to love her and all of us in no time.* With a smile on her face, she found herself wiping away a tear.

Facing the door of the restaurant, she was able to see Kristen enter and without her husband. That detail didn't bother her knowing he was still at work and Kristen agreed to meet her before she picked Isaiah up from football practice.

She sat up straight thinking perhaps that maybe today she'd follow her out, get in the car with her, and soon they would pull up to the side of a building and he'd come rushing out excited to see both of his moms.

But the latter of her thoughts were dismissed when she saw that familiar sadness in Kristen's eyes as she sat down across from her.

"Renee, how are you?"

Her face tensed. "I was a little hopeful until I just saw that look in your eyes. He still doesn't want to see me, does he?"

"I'm sorry, Renee, he doesn't. Like we told you, we won't pressure him to do it if he doesn't want to. Matter of fact, this week, he didn't even entertain the topic with us. He knows he can be open with us and tell us how he feels about anything, but he's starting to become withdrawn. I don't mind your calls, keeping you abreast with what's going on in his life, but constantly asking him about meeting you seems to be disturbing him. I just wanted to come here and say that we'll be laying off the subject with him for a while."

"But did you tell him that my sister died and that I need to meet him now more than ever? That I really love him, and I'm sorry for giving him up?"

"Yes, we have, but he's still adamant on not meeting you. Maybe he'll come around someday, maybe he won't." Kristen said with a sincerity she hoped didn't sound harsh.

Tears trekked Renee's face.

"I'm sorry, Renee. Like I said, you can keep in touch with me if you'd like and I'll give you updates as you ask. I hate that I can't stay longer, but I just remembered it's my turn to bring snacks for their game. I better get to the store and then over to his school. Take care." Kristen left just as quickly as she'd come.

Renee knew she wasn't supposed to condemn herself, but the thought of this all being her fault because she gave him away snuck up on her. She knew it was best if she left the restaurant before her immerging cryfest made a big scene and drew warranted stares her way.

She grabbed her purse and shifted on the bench, careful not to step on the hem of her long skirt when a tall figure stood in front of her and blocked her ability to get up from the table.

She dreaded looking up because his work boots didn't match the style of the waiters she'd scanned walking the restaurant since she'd been in it.

She slowly lifted her head and held her breath as she looked into the dark brown eyes of a man she hadn't seen in well over a decade. Since she'd given birth to their son and he was hauled off in handcuffs after beating her to near death. "Ted?" she uttered, not believing it was actually him.

One eyebrow lifted and he smirked as he peered at her. "Renee."

She froze. He said her name with such endearment that it disgusted her.

"Don't look so disappointed. I know I'm happy to see you. You look…so beautiful. Even better than when we were together." He offered his hand to help her get up.

She stared at its girth and remembered the strength of it the last time it went upside her head, balled into a fist and punched her in her stomach, her sides, anywhere he aimed on her body.

She wasn't that same woman he knew in undergrad; she knew she was stronger. Something inside of her wanted to scream for him to get away from her or kick him in the groin, but not wanting to make a scene, she abandoned that thought. She was readying herself to get up and walk past and away from him as soon as possible.

She stilled herself briefly, recalling that her last solution had never worked with him any other time he used her for a punching bag. But that didn't matter, she didn't want to cause a scene, but she'd finish what he started if he messed with her.

She scanned the table briefly, looking for a knife, some type of heavy object that could aid her in fighting off his bulk and strength if she needed to.

Noting the alarm in her eyes, he said, "Relax, I'm not going to do anything to you. I just want to talk."

"We have nothing to talk about." She stood up. She didn't want to be anywhere near him, but his proximity to her and the table left her no choice but to be almost face to chest with him. She didn't want to look up at him, but she didn't want her head low to insinuate that she was still afraid of him.

"Be easy." With a steady yet slow touch, he rubbed her jawline with the back of his calloused hand before dragging it down her face and forcing her head to lift. "After what I heard, we do need to talk."

He could see her balling her fists up, her chest heaving, and her jaw tensing.

"Relax," he said, holding his hands up high as if in surrender and taking one step back from her. "Please, just sit and let's talk for a minute."

Her arms flew up and across her chest as she leaned back into a defensive stance and trained her eyes on him. He didn't know it, but she wondered if she could actually break her jaw with as hard as she pressed her teeth together.

"Our son, that you're here trying to meet? We need to talk."

She stiffened knowing that he'd clearly overheard her conversation with Kristen, that he knew why she was in town, that their son was in D.C.

Her motherly instincts kicked in and a rage that she had never felt before overtook her, imagining him trying to exercise his paternal rights, him possibly hurting her son the way he did her. She charged at him, but just short of touching him. She lifted on her tiptoes and pointed her finger in his face as her nostrils flared. "If you even think about trying to reach out to him, do him the way you did me, I swear I'll kill you."

He smirked. "I see Kim rubbed off on you."

Him mentioning Kim made her want to slap him, hard. She would have had she not heard the clearing of a throat next to her.

Her waiter had returned to her table. "Is everything okay?"

She took a deep breath and looked at him, before looking back at Ted who had his hands raised and shoulders high as if he were innocent and unaware of why she was so volatile.

She took another deep, calming breath and looked back at the waiter. "Yes. I'm fine."

"Okay," he said, unconvinced. "Are you ready to order or heading out now?"

Order? She had no appetite, but wanting, hoping to set Ted straight, she said, "I'll sit and look over the menu again."

"Okay. I'll come back and check on you soon."

He walked away and Renee stepped backwards to her booth, never taking her eyes off Ted.

"Renee, I promise I won't do anything to you. You can ease up, tiger." He chuckled.

He soon sat down and their knees touched, making her scoot to the other end of her bench.

"Thanks for the leg room."

With her right hand, she gripped the utensils folded in a napkin on the table. Her eyes were trained on him. "So I wasn't paranoid, you have been following me? That was you I saw across the street from the antique store that day? Following me around in the museum earlier?"

"Yes."

"Why, and how are you even out?"

"That's irrelevant, the issue here is that you're back here trying to connect with our son. I want in on that, too."

"Never!" She snapped at him and jumped up from the table. "I will never let you see him, hurt him the way you did me." She stormed off.

"Renee, he's my son, too. This is ain't over." He yelled at her back as she fled the restaurant.

***

She made it back to her hotel and slammed the door behind her, securing every lock available. She looked through the peephole as she panted.

She had been looking over her shoulder, taking a longer route back to the hotel trying to make sure that he wasn't still following her. She knew Ted couldn't be trusted.

She hated how furious he had her and the fact that he'd terrified her because of his commanding presence. He had her crying again and that disgusted her. She thought those days were behind her.

Renee wanted to stay in D.C. longer to press the issue of finally meeting her son, but thrown off by her confrontation with Ted, she thought otherwise. When she calmed herself long enough to grasp her phone with her shaking hands, she called Andrew.

He answered and barely got in his greeting before she belted out, "I'm going back home, now."

10

Darius

"...so, like I was saying..." Darius found himself searching for the punchline to a joke for the fifth time that night.

He'd been on the tour going on a month. Judging from the laughs of the crowd each night, he'd been doing a pretty good job of entertaining them and keeping up the front that everything was alright with him in spite of missing Kim terribly. It was almost as if he was bi-polar. He joked and laughed onstage yet sat in the dark, tears brimming his eyes, and nursing a beer or shot of something whenever he wasn't onstage after his set.

Had it not been for the fellas and especially his phone conversation with Mrs. Williams the day before the tour started, he probably wouldn't have gone on it. That would've suited him fine, too, but he had to admit that the fifteen-minute set he did each night gave him a relief from his grief, because the loss he was feeling over Kim's death seemed to crush him at times.

Which is why the petite, caramel skinned, doe-eyed beauty sitting a few tables away from the stage was doing a number on his psyche. He had blinked so many times during his set trying to focus his deceiving eyes because she looked so much like Kim that he blamed his temporary eye disorder on the blinding peach colored shirt a hefty man wore sitting front and center of the stage.

The crowd soaked it up and filled the room with thundering laughter as he roasted the man for wearing such a bright colored, tight shirt given his girth.

Getting back to his distraction, it didn't help that the woman's hair color and length matched that of Kim's. She appeared to be as bold as Kim given she had been winking, licking her full lips, and adjusting in her seat to expose her thick thighs peeking from under her sweater dress for most of the time he stood on stage.

"That's my time, you all. Thank you and enjoy the rest of the show." He smiled as he saluted them and then handed the cordless mic to the host as he walked off the stage.

He was making his way to the back of the club that would lead to the backstage entrance when there was a slight tug on his arm. "Excuse me."

The soft, flowery smell of perfume matched the timber in the voice that interrupted him. He knew it was a woman.

Being much taller than her, he turned to look down at her and had to catch himself from jumping back in shock. She looked even more like Kim up close than she did from afar. He continued to stare at her without saying a word. How could he? He wasn't too sure what would come out. Should he be spooked about the resemblance or attracted to the fact that she looked so much like the woman he still loved?

"I'm sorry to bother you, but I wanted to catch you before you left. My name is Amber," she said, drawing closer to him as a corner of her mouth lifted into a sexy smirk.

He cleared his throat and stared at her a little longer before pulling himself together to speak. "My name is—"

"Darius, right?" She drew even closer to him, sticking her chest out knowing his height gave him the advantage of both looking at her face and the crests of her breasts. And although she too had round eyes, they lacked that fire he always saw in Kim's.

"Yes, nice to meet you, Amber." He kept his eyes on her face.

"The pleasure is all mine." She reached up and gripped his bicep, slowly rubbing her hand up and down it.

He cleared his throat again.

Her lids lowered and she licked her lips as her pointer finger beckoned him to lean down to hear her.

When he obliged, she leaned in to him, her lip intentionally grazing his ear as she whispered, "How about you and I get out of here?"

He pulled back from her and looked into her eyes trying to gauge if she was actually implying what he thought she was.

The nodding of her head and the want in her eyes left no room for misunderstanding.

He was stumped. The old Darius would've jumped at the chance to screw a fine woman such as herself, but the Darius who had just lost the love of his life a little over a month ago couldn't stomach being with another woman so soon after her death. He wasn't sure if he would ever love again, but the woman in front of him wasn't asking for love. Was she? It seemed she only wanted a one-night stand.

As he stared at her slowly licking her lips and pressing her body closer to his, he thought maybe he should give the night with her a shot. Maybe it'd get him out of the knowingly unhealthy funk he had been in.

"Let's go." He gripped her hand and led her out of the club, nodding to the tour manager on his way out.

Greg gave him a knowing nod as he exited the building.

***

Darius couldn't keep her hands off of him during their short walk from the comedy venue back to his hotel. He barely got his key in the slot before she began pulling at his clothes.

"Amber, wait, slow down."

"I didn't come here to talk, I come here to do you and that's exactly what I plan to do. Screw your brains out." She bunched his sweater up in her fist and pulled him into her, planting a wet kiss to his lips.

He immediately pulled back from her. She may have looked like Kim and her boldness may have even mirrored hers at some levels, but she definitely didn't kiss like Kim. Her kisses were sloppy, whereas Kim's were especially crafted in what he thought was just right for him.

Maybe he'd made a mistake bringing her there after all. Memories of being with Kim and the guilt of being with another woman was starting to settle in with him.

He braced his hands on her arms, putting distance between them. "Maybe we shouldn't do this."

"Oh, I think we should." She lurched forward again trying to kiss him, but his strength outdid hers and he gently pushed her back to an arms-length from him.

"I get it, you're not a kisser. That's okay, I know another place I can kiss to get you ready for the ride I'm about to take you on." She said with mischief dancing in her eyes as she slowly licked her lips.

What was it about him that made this woman want him so bad? He knew he was a good-looking man, but there were plenty other decent looking men in the club and yet she only seemed to have been focused on him. *Does she think I have money? About to hit big and think I'll be her cash cow?*

Darius was so lost in his musings that it wasn't until he felt the weight of his pants around ankles that he realized she'd made quick work of undoing his pants.

He felt her hand on his limp member. "Amber?" Staring at her, he cocked his head as if silently asking what she was doing.

"Don't worry, I see you're not ready yet, but I know how to change that." She winked. "I can only imagine how it'll be when all systems are go." She shimmied down his body, but he jumped back, causing him to fall on the bed.

"You wanna get more comfortable, I see." She jumped up and pounced on him, moaning and kissing on his neck as her hand inched down his body to grab him again, but his firm grasp on her arms and the sternness in his voice stilled her.

"Amber, I can't do this." He rolled from up under her, stood up and began to fully clothe himself again. "What's wrong?" She asked, her doe eyes looking like big saucers filled with worry.

"It's not you, it's me. I thought I could do this, but I can't."

"What, are you saying I'm not good enough for you?" Her voice elevated and her eyes narrowed in on him as she sat up in the bed.

He shook his head. "No, it's nothing like that. I was in a relationship that ended suddenly and tragically."

"Oh." Her face softened and her hands fell to her sides. "I'm sorry to hear that," she said as she began to gather her things, "but I was all up on you for a minute and your friend still wasn't ready to play, you really may not be ready." She walked to the door and turned to look at him one last time. "Goodbye, Darius."

The door closed softly behind her and Darius looked down at his flattened zipper. She was right. As hot as she was in her dress, her hooded eyes and caresses boldly saying what she was willing to do to him, and yet his manhood still hadn't come to life.

"Was it her or was it me?" He plopped down on the bed and fell back, contemplating the answers to his questions.

11

Pam

"Man up and tell her already," Vance mumbled to himself as he closed the door to his house. At that point, he didn't know which was worse, not having told Pam about the offer to lead Memphis' school district or it having been over a month since the offer was presented to him and he still hadn't told her.

Either way, he knew she'd be vexed over it all, but he still had to tell her. They needed to discuss it. For as much as he wanted the position, he knew marriage was a partnership, not a dictatorship. He couldn't just storm in there and tell her that they were moving to another state, start a new life, and she better had deal with it.

Nope.

He knew that wouldn't work with a strong woman like Pam. Besides, he wouldn't do that anyway. He loved her too much and wanted her to be happy and comfortable with whatever decision they made together.

He still wasn't ready for the talk, but he knew he had to because the chatter about him taking the position had started to rev up in the district office and with the way the gossipers pulled the grapes from the vine, it was a wonder to him how someone hadn't already let it slip to her about the offer and the presumption that he'd automatically take the position. "Pam, sweetie, where are you?"

"In the kitchen," she said from the back of the house.

The sun had set and the house was dim save the candle lights he could see flickering in the kitchen. He loosened his tie and undid the top button of his dress shirt as he crossed over into the kitchen.

He smiled wide seeing his gorgeous wife seated at the candlelit table in the breakfast nook of their kitchen.

"What's this for?" he asked as he passed what he knew was his seat in front of a plate filled with pasta, pan-seared chicken breasts, and asparagus. He rounded the table and bent over. He slowly grazed her face with his fingertips before lifting her chin and bringing her lips up to meet his.

The kiss was slow and tender at first, but he wasn't satisfied with the sweetness of it. He pulled her up to her feet, wrapped one arm around her waist as his other hand palmed the back of her head and played in her hair.

His actions caused her to moan and lift on her tiptoes as he pulled her flush to him and explored her mouth with an urgency, a fervor, that suggested he was hungry for something other than what was on the table. "We can skip dinner and get right to dessert." He pulled away from her mouth just enough to make his words intelligible, but soon nipped at her bottom lip and then sucked her tongue in his mouth as his hands traveled south and gripped the roundness of her firm backside.

"No." She hesitantly pulled back from him and playfully hit his chest. "We should eat first."

"Oh, I plan to eat." He leaned back in to kiss her and she obliged him with a quick peck on his lips, then pointed to his seat. "You need to take that, sir. We need to talk."

And just like that, the bubble of bliss he had tried to cocoon them in when they were kissing had popped.

He didn't move to his seat yet but stared at her pert mouth and her slanted dark brown eyes, trying to see any sign of her knowing about the offer and being mad at him, but her features were just as neutral as they were when he entered the kitchen.

"Okay. We can eat what you cooked first, but I'm having you as my dessert afterwards." He squeezed her butt and she giggled as she pushed him in the direction of his seat.

They sat and she stared at him devouring his food. She didn't know why she was on edge waiting to talk to him.

Yes, she did.

She knew exactly why it felt like her heart was about to burst. She was so overcome with what she knew, but first things first, she needed him to fess up about the job offer.

She shouldn't have let a whole month go by without saying something to him about it. She'd planned to address him the same day she accidentally overheard the conversation at work, but she'd ended up having an hour-long conversation with Monica and Renee that night. When Vance came home and said nothing to her about it, she'd calmed down enough to reason she would let him bring it up to her. Especially since she shouldn't have overheard the conversation anyway, but a month had been too long for the secret to still exist between them.

She'd make him come clean so that she could come clean with an omission of her own.

His plate was almost empty when he finally looked up at her; really, it was to grab his glass of water, but they made eye contact nonetheless.

He cleared his throat as he wiped his mouth before pushing his plate away from him. He looked at her and looked back at his empty plate. "I'm sorry for pretty much eating alone, not paying you any attention. I was just so hungry and you know you can throw down in the kitchen." He winked.

"Mmh hmmm," she said, smirking, with a raised eyebrow.

"You can." He scooted back from the table and patted his thigh. "Come here."

Pam hesitated briefly before looking at her handsome husband and sashaying over to sit on his lap, be closer to him. She settled in his lap as he wrapped his arms around her waist.

"So, how was your day?" He kissed her chin. "I barely saw you at work."

"I know. You're so busy being the boss, we don't see each other unless you come to my classroom or we have a staff meeting."

"That's because you've yet to take me up on my standing offer to come to my office for a quickie."

She playfully hit him on his arm.

"What?" He pulled her in closer to him. "You know I have a bathroom in there. We can go in it, lock the door, and get busy at work. I say that's a win-win for both of us."

"You are so silly."

"But I ain't joking. I be wanting you when I see you at work. We gotta do it there at least once." His bright eyes widened with excitement and a slight pout formed on his ever so kissable lips.

She pursed her lips as she stared at him before putting her hand flat on his chest and tried to push away from him, but he held her tightly.

"How about here and now?" He leaned in, puckering.

She leaned back far as if she were preparing for a backbend.

He shook his head at her and chuckled before helping her up some.

"Stop resisting and you won't find yourself in another comprising situation, although I'd like to put you in one, legs behind your head?" His eyebrows wriggled.

"Stop, silly. We need to talk." She pried herself away from his firm grasp of her and stood in front of him. Not knowing how to say it or even what to say first, she wrung her hands together.

"Pam, baby, what's wrong?" He grabbed her by her hips, pulling her close to him.

She pushed off him, creating distance between them. The last time she'd tried to confront him about it, she caved in to his kiss and their all-night lovemaking session. But she wouldn't let the coveted chemistry between them hinder her from finally hearing the truth from him.

"What's wrong is, I think you have something to tell me. Been keeping it to yourself for a while."

Vance froze. *Does she know about the job offer? But how? Ole gossiping teachers.* He shook his head and stood to his full six-foot two height.

He walked towards her with an empathetic look of sorrow on his face. "Baby."

"Don't baby me. Do you have something to tell me?" One brow lifted as he slowly approached her.

"Yes, but—" He tried to pull her close to him, but she evaded his grasp and circled around him so she wouldn't be sandwiched between him and the kitchen island.

"So, it's true. You're taking the job in Memphis?"

His head dropped as he braced his hands on the countertop and let out a loud sigh.

"Say something."

He turned to face her and knew his night wouldn't end well. She stood with one leg out in front of the other. Her foot tapped meticulously while her arms were firmly folded across her chest. Although short in stature, she was never short on standing her ground when she reached her boiling point. He could tell she was at it given the tightness of her mouth pressed together and the beady focus of her eyes on him.

"This is not how I wanted to tell you."

"I can't tell. You've let a whole month go by and not tell me anything."

Now his eyebrow lifted. "I've known longer than a month. Who told you? How did you find out?"

Her stare softened and her hands dropped to her sides as she mumbled, "I overheard you talking to the COO in your office after work one day."

"Hunh?" He walked towards her with a slight smirk on his face. "So, you were eavesdropping?"

"No? I wasn't. I mean, I didn't mean to. You know how close our mailboxes are to the backdoor of your office. I was walking away from it, out of the office and headed to my car when I heard the conversation." She mumbled the last of her words as her head tilted.

"So, eavesdropping?" He smiled, trying to lighten up the moment as he reached to pull her towards him, but she shooed his hands away.

"Stop joking. This is serious. You accepted a job in another state and didn't even talk to me about it?" Her fury was shifting to hurt.

"No, I would never do that." He sat down on one of the dark wood chairs and after a bit of tugging, coaxed her into sitting on his lap again.

Still, she folded her arms across her chest.

"Aww, don't be that way with me." He nibbled on her bottom lip.

She swatted him a few times before he finally stopped trying to kiss her.

He took a deep breath and said, "They came to me with the offer the day after Kim passed in the hospital."

She stiffened.

He rubbed her back.

"Of course, I paid it no mind considering what had just happened. But as the days went by, the Board of Ed for Memphis began to contact me via phone and whatnot and soon, so did our district. At first, Mr. Hubert was wanting to keep me here to use me to replicate my system across the city, but Memphis assured them that if I took the job there and was successful, the praise would go to it being a Chicago initiative. With Memphis being a smaller yet troubled district and willing to pay for the plan, our Board readily agreed not to put in an offer to convince me to stay here, yet."

"So, there's a chance you can stay here and be promoted?" Her voice filled with hope.

He grimaced and cocked his head to the side. "You know how the politics are when it comes to the Board of Ed here in Chicago. Let's just say I wouldn't hold my breath waiting for that offer. They just want to use this promotion to milk it for the national exposure it would get."

"So you're going to take it?" Her hands flew up as her voice elevated.

"Pam, I didn't say that. I was just catching you up on everything. You know I want the promotion because of what I'd get to do with the position. I'd be able to reform an entire school district thereby improving the quality of education for thousands of students, hopefully shifting their life's outcome, but you know I would never make a decision like that without you." He gently gripped her chin, turning her face towards his.

"I didn't wanna keep it from you, but baby, you were dealing with Kim passing and Renee trying to reunite with her son. I didn't wanna burden you with anything else."

"So when do you have to give them the final answer?"

"Like yesterday."

"Vance, I can't leave the sisterhood at a time like this and my mother and my relationship is better than ever. I don't wanna leave her, plus I'll need her help with the…"

"With the what? What's wrong?" he asked as she jumped up from his lap with her hand covering her mouth. She ran straight to the half bathroom nearby.

"Pam, Pam." He ran after her and made it to the bathroom door just as it slammed in his face.

Pam couldn't respond to him or his knocking, she was too busy throwing up.

"You throwing up in there? Think it was the food?"

She stood up from her temporary porcelain home and tuned the faucet on. She looked at herself in the mirror between splashing her face with water. "No, Vance, it wasn't the food," she said out loud knowing the running water and his knocks on the door provided a sound barrier between him hearing her. "It wasn't the food."

12

Monica

Monica had bid her time long enough with Keith, three whole months to be exact. But today, she decided she had to put an end to his sulking, at least when it came to neglecting her and the kids.

It was late, after nine p.m. She heard him finally come in and knew he went straight to his home office when she heard the door close. Asleep in their beds already, she gave the twins one last kiss before she turned off the main light, leaving a bright Mickey Mouse night light softly illuminating the room. She gently closed the door behind her.

She rubbed her protruding belly and whispered, "It'll be okay you two. You'll get the same attention in utero your older brother and sister were given by your dad soon enough." She held the bannister all the way down the stairs.

Her fluffy slipper clad feet dragged against the dark stained hardwood floors as she made her way down the short hallway that led to his office. She made it to his door and said a quick, silent prayer to herself that she would get through to him this time rather than strangle him as she wanted to in past times. Per his knew behavior, whenever she brought up the subject to him, he stormed out of the house claiming he needed fresh air or had work to do.

She took a deep breath and twisted the door knob. It didn't open. "Keith, unlock this door and let me in."

She tried to pace her breathing as she felt her temper rise, but when she didn't hear any movement on the other side of the door, she began to bang on it. "Keith Jabari Williams Sr., open this door right now before I break it down."

"Monica, I'm working," he yelled from the other side.

She opened her mouth to say something in protest but thought against it. Just when she was walking away to find something that might help her ram into the door to gain entry, it pulled open.

"Monica?"

She stared at him with her head cocked to the side. "Don't Monica me." She pushed him aside and made her way into his office.

Still holding onto the door knob, he dropped his head and sighed. "Monica, I have work I need to finish," he said with his back facing her.

"Keith, right now, I couldn't care less what you need to do for work. You have a family you have been neglecting for months and that stops now." Her voice shook.

Through it all, it was never his desire to ignore her, he just couldn't shake the way he felt about losing Kim. It made him withdraw from everyone. She thought he was ignoring her, but burying himself in his work was all he could do to keep strong and not completely break down in front of her, lose it all together. What good would he be then if he couldn't go to work, make money, and provide for his family?

"Keith, look at me!" she screamed.

The tremble in her voice made him slowly turn to look at his wife. His beautiful, glowing wife carrying a life he helped her produce. He could see pain all over her face and surmised he was a major cause of it.

"Monica, what do you want me to do?" He moved a few paces and sat on the ledge of his desk.

"What I want you to do is to be my husband, my best friend. We're supposed to be in this together." Her voice softened.

"Monica," he choked on his tears, "I can't do this. I don't know how to get past losing her." He buried his face in one hand trying to muffle his sobs.

She walked over to him and began to rub his back. "For one, quit trying to be so strong and not deal with it. This hasn't been easy for any of us, but we can't shut each other out. Especially not how you've been doing me." She playfully punched him. "I know you're grieving and everyone does it differently, but I swear you've made me so mad this past month.

"You don't play with the kids, you don't talk to me, at all, you don't touch me. Do you know how horny I've been this trimester? Ooo, I could strangle you for all of the nights you've turned your back on me in bed or didn't even come to bed."

"What do you want me to do?" He kept his head low. He didn't want her to see him crying.

"Talk to me about how you really feel." She rubbed his back.

"I'm not ready to."

"Keith, you have to deal with this. You're gonna grieve whether you deal with it or not. You just need to do it in a healthy way. Maybe you should see a therapist, a grief counselor."

His back erected and he stared at her. "I said I don't want to talk about it at all and your solution is for me to go see a therapist? I just need to deal with this in my own way."

His defensive stance enraged her. The interaction had been too much for her emotions. One minute it seemed as if she was getting through to him, and the next, he retreated. She needed to get away from him and cool off. "Well, you better do something fast because you have toddler twins, a wife, and two more babies on the way that need a loving husband and father. I didn't sign up to do this alone." She stormed off, slamming the door behind her.

Keith stared at the closed door before he charged at it and punched it, blowing out a loud breath. Soon, his shoulders slumped as his head braced against the door. He knew his wife was right. He needed to get help, he just didn't know if talking about his triplet's death would help him begin to heal or fully unravel him.

13

Renee

"Yes, I just landed," Renee said into her phone as she waited in baggage claim at the airport.

"Well, who's there to get you? Why didn't you even tell us you were coming back so soon? When we three talked on the phone earlier this week, you said you were going to stay there until you met with him. Did it happen? Why didn't you tell us about it?"

"Pam, would you take a breath, please? I didn't meet with him. And I just…I just decided to come back yesterday."

It seemed like it would be the perfect time to tell the real reason that sent her rushing back home, Ted's sudden appearance. She knew the sisterhood had agreed to not hold anymore secrets from one another ever again, but she still needed to process his resurgence in her life. And him threatening that he wanted to see their son infuriated her to no end. She would tell them soon, just not yet. Besides, she'd tell Pam and Monica together, telling one before the other might hurt the one told last feelings. She'd keep her encounter with him at the restaurant to herself for the time being.

"Renee, are you still there?"

"Yeah." Renee shook her head realizing she'd gotten so lost in thought that she must've missed some of what Pam had said. "Yeah, I'm still on the phone." She bit her nail and stared at the transitioning flight info on the carousel next to her.

"Well, why didn't you call someone so we could be there to pick you up? I know you didn't leave your car parked there since you've been gone. It's cold outside. You taking public transportation, or is Andrew coming to get you? Your parents? Because if not, I'm on my lunch break, but if you give me a second, I'm certain I can get the in-house sub to cover my class for the rest of the day and I come get you."

"Pam." Given her outburst, Renee turned her back to the small crowd of people staring at her. She lowered her voice. "Pam, I'm okay. My luggage just came up on the carousel and my phone shows an Uber is pulling up as we speak. I'm known to be the worry-wart, not you. What has you up in arms? Is everything okay?"

"I'm okay." The lie flew out of her mouth before she even had the chance to consider it. She wasn't okay. She still hadn't told Vance about her situation and she knew it wasn't best to tell Renee and Monica before she told her husband. Her secret had kept her antsy the past couple of days, maybe that's why she hadn't let Renee get a word in edge-wise.

She definitely couldn't share that Vance was considering taking a job in another state. That would be too much for them to handle knowing another one of them would essentially be leaving the crew. But even those things didn't amount to her current worry. She was most concerned about Renee suddenly popping up back home with no notice and not having met her son yet, something she knew Renee desperately wanted to happen.

"I don't get why you're back if you didn't meet him. That was the whole reason for you taking a leave of absence from work."

"Pam, I'm allowed to come home," she said as she got into the back of the Uber.

"I know, sweetie. You are and I'm so glad you're back. I've missed you and worried about you so much. Where are you headed to now? I'll come straight there when I get off work."

"I'm gonna head to Monica and Keith's now. I'll make my way to my parent's house later."

"No Andrew?" Pam asked in a whimsical tone and wriggled her eyebrows as if Renee could see her expression.

Renee smiled, something she hadn't done since before she had dinner with Kristen the day before. Andrew always seemed to make her smile. "I'm certain he'll be over there with me later. He would've come to pick me up, tried to push back a meeting with a client to do so, but I wouldn't let him. Seems like he's sacrificed so much of his time on me already since we've been together."

"And there's nothing wrong with that. You're worth the sacrifice. Do I need to go Kim on you and remind you that you're worthy of his attention and affection?" Pam snipped with a hint of humor in her voice.

Renee's smile sobered up at the mention of Kim's name. Imagining how she'd get on her for not demanding more of Andrew's time, soak in all of the love he tried to shower on her, made her smile return. She rolled her eyes as if Pam could see her. "No, Mother, you don't. I know I deserve love, his love. I just try not to be inconsiderate of his time. He has a life. He's put off so many meetings, switched to teleconferences just to be in D.C. with me, to be by my side.

"I'm grateful for it and I love him being there, but I know I have to be supportive of him too. As a sports agent, his clients depend on him to make the connections and broker their deals. I don't want him to lose them and then he resent me for the time he spent with me rather than doing his job keeping his clients happy and taking care of their business."

"I hear ya and it's good you think that way. Most women don't understand that a man with a lot of money like Andrew means that he spends hours trying to keep it and make more. Kim would be proud of you, thriving in your relationship and all."

The line went silent. They both knew why. Kim had been brought up one too many times in their short conversation in the past tense.

"Renee?"

"Yeah?" Renee said barely audible.

"I'm sorry for bringing her up so much. I'm just still not use to her not being around. We would've already made plans to crash Mon's house by sundown to catch up with you and what happened in D.C."

"I know. I'm still trying to process it, too. Well, I just pulled up to Mon's and I'm about to get out. I'll talk to you later."

"You sure will. I'll call you when I'm on my way to your parents. I've missed you."

I've missed you, too," Renee said.

Soon, Renee was at Monica's door with her big suitcase and a fake smile on her face. She had a show to put on. She had to appear as if she'd only come back home because she missed everyone and needed to regroup before she tried again at connecting with her son and not because she ran back home shook and infuriated with her encounter with Ted.

She raised her hand to ring the bell, but the door opened wide and quick and a round-bellied Monica snatched her smaller frame into her arms. She hugged her for quite some time before pulling back and looking into her face. "I've missed you. I've missed your face." Monica plastered a kiss on Renee's cheek.

"I've missed you, too."

Monica stepped aside to let Renee in. "Here, let me get that for you." Monica leaned forward to grab the handle to Renee's suitcase, but Renee shooed her hand away.

"Missy, I can manage this suitcase. You on the other hand, and I hate to say it, have grown much rounder since I last saw you. It's amazing how the human body works. It took you longer to show with the twins than it did with that one bun in your oven."

"Well, maybe that's because the first two prepped me for these two. Carved out a camping site for them."

The wheels on the plaid roller board stopped spinning. "Two? Them?" Renee turned an inquisitive stare to Monica.

"Yes, two." Monica slowly nodded her head as a slight smile graced her face.

"Oh my goodness, Mon. That's great. I'll have four nieces and nephews soon." She scurried over to Monica and hugged her. Pulling back from her, she said, "I bet you Keith is over the moon about it too. He always did want a big family."

At the mention of her husband, she burst out crying. She shimmied from Renee's grasp and made her way into the den.

She began mumbling, picking up the twins' toys, straightening throw pillows, pretty much doing anything to ignore her cries.

Renee quickly hung her coat on the rack at the door, took her shoes off, and rushed to Monica. She moved around the pacing pregnant woman until she was in front of her and grabbed her hands, forcing her to stop. "Monica, what's wrong, sweetie?"

Eyes red and mouth filled with sobs, Monica looked up at Renee. "Everything is wrong."

Renee began to rub circles on Monica's back, hoping to soothe her as she led her over to the couch.

"Like what?" Renee squeezed Monica's hand.

"Like Kim is gone and she's never coming back and because of that, I think I've lost your brother."

"What?" Renee's eyebrows furrowed as she stared at her sister-in-law.

"We barely speak, Renee. He ignores me and the kids, works late, and when he does come home, he hides in the office until it's time for him to go to work again. You know I found out I was having twins by myself?"

Monica looked at Renee as if waiting for an answer but then continued on. "He knew about the appointment but didn't show up. Said he had a meeting, but that's not how it always is. As head of his department, he can take days off, work from home, or reschedule things as needed. He chose not to be there with me."

Renee couldn't believe what she was hearing. It's not that she thought her brother could do no wrong, it was more so knowing how long Keith loved Monica before they got together. How he adored her and loved their kids. Keith was the model family man, so to hear how he had been behaving was alarming, baffling to her.

"Yes, your brother Keith has been behaving like an—"

Renee held up her hand hoping to stall the expletive she could see dancing on the tip of Monica's tongue. "Don't get out of character over him."

Monica wiped at her face. "I've been trying to be patient with him but he infuriates me and it hurts all at the same time. It's like I've lost two best friends instead of just one, Renee." Monica's vision blurred from tears pooling her eyes.

"I'm sorry. Have you talked to him about how you feel?"

"Talked to him about it?" Monica snapped her neck at Renee. "Talked to him about it? Yes, I've tried that, Renee, and maybe if he talked back to me, I wouldn't feel the way I do. I feel so alone in this." Monica wrapped her arms around herself and cried harder than she had since the funeral.

Although she hadn't planned to come back until after she had met her son and they were on their way to building a relationship, she was glad that she was back, because clearly her friends and family needed her there. "Monica, sweetie, let's do what I know works, pray."

Renee rested her chin on Monica's shoulder and rubbed her back as she prayed words of comfort and peace into Monica's ear and hopefully into her spirit.

Monica's cries began to subside.

"You need something to drink, sweetie?"

Monica merely nodded her head.

"Okay, I'll go get you some water."

"No, that's okay," she spoke up, not wanting Renee to keep fussing over her. "I can go get it myself." She braced her hand on the arm of the couch to stand, but Renee gripped her other wrist.

"No, you just sit there. I'll go get it." Monica conceded with the nod of her head and Renee got up from the couch and was headed towards the kitchen when she heard the front door open.

She looked to her left to see Keith enter and slowly close the door behind him. His head hung low and he looked drained and worn-out, even from the distance she stood from him. She watched as he took his shoes off and threw his pea coat on the rack at the front door, not even bothering to pick it up when it fell to the floor.

His feet dragged across the floor as he attempted to walk past her without even speaking.

Him not acknowledging her presence stunned her. He always made it his business to greet her and Kim with a kiss or a hug especially when they had been physically apart from each other as long as she had been in D.C. Come to think of it, Keith hadn't called her once when she was in D.C.

"Excuse you?" Her voice was sharp and her eyes were wide.

"Hey, Renee," he mumbled and kept walking past her to his office.

Renee hurried her steps and rushed to get in front of him before he could make it to his office door. Finally seeing Monica's description of this new Keith, she could see that he was intent on getting in and locking the door, leaving her on the other side of it. "Excuse you."

"I said hey, Renee."

"No, it's more than a hey. We need to talk."

"Renee, I have work to do."

"Monica tells me that you're ignoring her and the kids. What's up with that?"

He stopped and looked at her. "I've never known you to get in people's business like this."

"Well, that used to be Kim's job, but she's not around, so maybe I have to step into that role a bit. Especially when it comes to my brother ignoring my sister-in-law and my niece and nephew."

He cocked his head and looked at her. "Renee, get out of the way."

"No, we need to talk."

"Renee, I said move."

"No."

His forearm extended out and pushed her out of the way as he walked through his office door. He tried to close the door behind him, but she pressed her body against it.

"Keith, you pushed me."

He didn't look back at her. He knew he was wrong for pushing her, but he just didn't feel like talking to her. Her mentioning that Kim was gone and she'd have to take her role annoyed him. Kim was supposed to be alive and her feisty in-your-business self. Renee was supposed to be quiet and slightly naïve and he could be the protective brother. He at least wanted to right his wrong of pushing her.

"I'm sorry, but I really have a project that I need to finish. I'm glad you're back and I'll catch up with you soon. Now can you please close the door behind you so I can get this work done?"

She ignored his request and stepped in and closed the door behind her. "No, we need to talk. I know how long you loved Monica and what it took for you all to get together. Remember how crazy you were when she refused to marry you because she thought she couldn't have kids and didn't want to hold you back from having the family you wanted?"

He said nothing.

Renee continued, "But you pursued her until she said yes and married you. Now, look. You all have two beautiful babies and she's pregnant with twins again and you're not even here to support her the way that I know that you can." Her voice softened. "Is it because Kim is gone?"

His fists balled up and he took in a deep breath, trying to calm himself. He actually hated people even mentioning her name.

She could see his jaw tightening. She went on the side of him and wrapped her arm around his waist. "Keith, we were triplets. I'm hurting just as bad as you are, but you know and I know that anger is not the way to deal with any of this. We were raised to have faith in God and to believe that He will see us through anything.

"And although it hurts so bad, I'm trying to hold on to that faith because that's the only way I'm going to be able to make it through. Keith, that's the only way I'm going to be able to meet my son and build a relationship with him is by putting my faith and trust in God. He knows what's best and has my back no matter what."

Keith looked down at her. He couldn't see her face, but he could tell she was crying against his chest. "Did you get to meet him?"

"No."

He found himself wrapping his arm around her and gripping her. "I'm sorry you didn't meet him yet. I know that's what you really want."

"I don't have my son yet, but you have your wife and you have your kids. You have to be here for them. You have to open up to Monica. Don't let whatever you're not dealing with drive a wedge between you all."

"Renee, that's really not any of your business."

"Yes, it is." She stepped back from him to look him in the eyes. "You are my business. And now that Kim is gone, we have to be there for one another even more so than ever."

He turned his back to walk away from her, but she ran and hopped in front of him and put her arms around him again. "You have to find a different way to deal with your grief. If you don't want to talk to your wife or me or Mom and Dad about it, then you have to go see somebody about it. You have to get right and make things better for you and for your family."

She didn't think there was any more that she could say at that point. He was right, she wasn't Kim. As much as she wanted to say something to convince him to snap out of it, she wasn't as quick-witted and sharp with her tongue as Kim was. She kissed him on the cheek and left out of his office, closing the door behind her. She said a quick prayer to herself that he would do what he needed to do to get right for his family.

Just then, her phone vibrated. Although her vision was blurry because of the tears she shed during her quick prayer, she could clearly see Andrew's handsome, chiseled face on the screen. She accepted the call. "Hello."

"Hey, beautiful. Where are you?"

"I'm at Monica's. How are you?"

"I'm good, but you're not good. I can tell you've been crying. I'm on my way over there."

"No, please." She held her hand up in protest as if he could see her. "I'm going to head to my parents now. Just meet me over there."

"Well, how are you going to get over there?"

"I'll take an Uber." She rubbed her temple trying to assuage the onslaught of a headache.

"Renee, you don't have to take an Uber when I can easily come get you."

"Drew, you are so sweet and I appreciate all that you try to do for me, but I'll be okay with the twenty to thirty-minute ride to my parents' house. Just meet me over there. You know that you have so much to do for your clients so don't rush whatever you're doing just for me. I know that you're a working man. I'll see you when you get over there."

He let out a sigh. "You are so stubborn when it comes to me being there for you, but okay. I love you."

She smiled. "I love you, too. Bye." She wiped her face and eased her way back down the hallway until she made it to Monica still sitting on the couch. Her face was dry, but it was apparent that she had been crying and she looked distraught.

Renee remembered that she needed to get Monica some water. She rushed back into the kitchen, grabbed a bottle of water, and went back to Monica still sitting alone in the dim living room. "Here, sweetie," she said, sitting down next to her. "Are you going to be okay by yourself, or do you want me to stay here with you?"

"Thank you for everything, Renee, but I'll be fine. I have no choice but to be fine. I have to be strong for me and my babies. I'm trying to be strong for my husband, too." She sighed. "You go on and see your parents and we'll catch up soon. I want to know everything that happened in D.C."

Renee averted eye contact with Monica. She didn't need her face to tell that there was something she wasn't telling her. She couldn't stay in the house any longer than she needed to because if one thing was certain about The Sisterhood, they could tell when each other were holding back. She wouldn't dare release her burden on Monica, given what she was dealing with concerning her brother. She cleared her throat. "Okay."

She looked down at her phone and pressed submit for an Uber. "Let me put my shoes and coat back on. It says an Uber is a minute away. I'll talk to you later. Love you." She gave Monica a long, endearing hug and then stood up to go get dressed to go back out into the cold winter of Chicago.

She got into the back of the small sedan and aimlessly stared out the window until it pulled up in front of her parents' ranch style home in the neighboring suburb.

"Thank you," she said to the driver as she got out and struggled with getting her bag out of the trunk. The young driver was so focused on texting someone that she didn't even bother to help Renee. She pulled off the minute she felt the trunk close.

Renee stretched the handle out to roll her bag up to her parents' front door. She hadn't bothered to call and let them know that she was coming, but it wouldn't matter if they were there or not since she had a key to let herself in. She'd just go to her old room and camp out there for a while. She wasn't ready to go back to her apartment anytime soon.

By the time she made it up to the porch, the door opened and her father stood there smiling at her.

"Welcome back home, baby girl," her dad said and reached out and grabbed her bag from her. He pulled it and her into him and gave her a long, firm hug before he pulled back and kissed her cheek. He leaned back to get a good look at her again and then leaned in to kiss her again. "Come on and get out of this cold." He moved her up and closed the door behind them.

"Hi, Daddy," she said, looking at him.

"We didn't expect you back so soon, sweetie. You met him?"

"No, sir, I didn't. Where's Mom?" Renee couldn't help the sadness in her voice.

Her father let out a long sigh. "She's laying down, resting."

"What's wrong?"

"One of her episodes of losing Kim. She hasn't gotten out of bed in days."

Renee's eyes widened. "Dad, why didn't you tell me? I would have come home sooner."

"I knew what you were there doing, baby. We know this is something you need to do. Besides, I'm here. I've been taking good care of her as best as I can, but there's nothing that you can give a mother after losing a child, just your presence and space if need be."

Renee took her coat and shoes off and left them at the front door. She stuffed her hands into the pockets of her long jean skirt and made a slow walk down the hall that lead to her parents' bedroom. She stood in the doorway for a second staring at her mother bawled up under the covers. She inched near the bed to see her mother, who was always so strong and full of life, looking lifeless, laying on her side sniffling.

The bed shifted and squeaked a little as Renee's body slowly crept across it until she was on her side and in front of her mother. Roberta opened her arms and Renee shifted until her mother's embrace engulfed her.

She took in a deep breath, inhaling her mom's scent. Roberta always smelled of the sweetest flowers. Being so close to her mother made it feel like that's where she belonged.

Soon her tears mixed in with her mother's and they laid there silently for a while.

"Mom?"

"Yes, sweetie," Roberta said, barely above a whisper.

"I'm sorry that you're hurting, but like you taught me, earth has no sorrow that heaven cannot heal."

"I know, baby. I know. It's just not right for a parent to outlive their child." She gripped Renee tighter. "I've missed you." She kissed her forehead. "How are you?"

"I'm as good as I can be."

"Did you meet him?"

"No, ma'am, not yet." Renee snuggled closer to her mother.

Roberta rubbed Renee's back again. "I'm sorry. I know you really wanted to meet him. Will you keep trying?"

"Yes, ma'am. I'll never stop trying."

"Good, we just have to have faith that everything will work out according to God's perfect will for our lives. I'm so proud of you." She smiled and rubbed Renee's cheek.

"Why? I messed up and had a baby out of wedlock with an abusive man and was forced to give my son up for adoption."

"None of that matters. That was your past and the abuse was not your fault. You're so sensitive and caring. You turned out to be a strong woman of God. That's what makes me so proud of you. As traumatizing as it was for you, that past you just brought up is what helped to make you who you are right now. A beautiful, selfless, and loving woman. That's why I'm proud of you."

Renee moved in closer to her mother and squeezed her tighter. "I love you so much, Mom. And I miss her so much, too." Renee's body heaved and she openly sobbed.

Roberta did the same to the point where you couldn't tell where one's cries ended and the others began.

Mr. Williams came in and sat on the bench at the foot of the bed and rubbed his wife's feet. "It's going to be okay, baby." He patted his daughter's legs. "It's going to be okay. We'll all get through this."

Renee lay next to her mother until she heard her soft snores. She looked down to see her father stand up and stretch.

"You going to stay here tonight, or you going home?"

"I planned on staying here, but Andrew should be coming over soon so I may go out with him or we may just hang out in the living room. If that's okay with you?" she said in a low voice hoping not to wake her mother. She peeled away from her mother and lifted from the bed as quietly as she could.

"You know that's fine with me." Her father kissed her before she walked out of the door.

The minute she left her parents' room, her phone vibrated and Andrew's face appeared on her screen. She cleared her throat before she answered. "Hi."

He paused for a second. "I swear I wish I could take all of your pain away from you. I hate seeing you like this and knowing that you're not at your jolly and upbeat best."

She smiled. "I'm okay. I was just laying down with my mother."

"I'm on my way to your parents. Is that cool?"

"Yes. See you soon."

"Bet."

She ended the call and her growling stomach led her to the kitchen. Crossing the threshold, she paused. *When was the last time I ate?* She couldn't even remember the last time she had eaten. She had been so shaken over Ted that she only worried herself with getting back home. Pam, Monica, and her time just spent with her mother had consumed her since she'd gotten back.

It hit her that she hadn't eaten in close to a day.

She walked over to the refrigerator and decided to whip up something so that there would be enough for her mother to eat when she finally decided to get out of bed. She would make enough for her dad as well.

She was busy warming up the cans of soup that she had found in the cabinets when the doorbell rang.

She made her way to answer it but stopped in front of the mirror in the hallway to check her appearance. She frowned, not liking what she saw, but it was the best that she could probably look at the moment, given the fact that she had been crying majority of the day.

She smoothed her bushy eyebrows out as Kim would have done knowing she was about to meet her man. She wiped her face one last time and patted her hair as she made her way down the hallway. She took a deep breath and opened the door.

Her breath caught in her throat looking at the most handsome man that she had ever seen before. She never tired of admiring his smooth chocolate skin. The moment was made so much more special with the way he stared back at her. It seemed like he always only had eyes for her.

"Hi, Drew," she said in a girlish voice that she didn't even know was hers.

"Hi, beautiful." He stepped through the door and grabbed her up in his arms. His clothes were cold from the outside elements, but it didn't matter because his hug was so warm, so protective, so strong that she rested in his arms until the draft from outside forced them to break apart long enough for him to step in and close the door.

Once the draft was no longer a nuisance for them, he pulled her back in his arms, kissing her forehead, her cheek, before he touched her chin and tilted her head up to stare into her eyes. "I've missed you so much."

Her eyes smiled as much as her lips curved upward. "It's only been a couple of days since we last saw each other."

"A couple of days too long." He looked in her eyes with an unmeasured tenderness before he leaned down to place a soft, slow, lingering kiss to her naturally pouty lips.

She thought it would be a simple kiss, but it turned into a smoldering hot collision of their lips that had Renee pushing him off her. Her eyes widened as she looked at him. "Drew," she took a breath, "I told you that we can't kiss like that."

He laughed. "Renee, I told you I won't go beyond kissing you."

"I told you I'm not scared of you, I'm scared of me."

He laughed again. "You're so silly," he said as he took his coat off and hung it on the coat rack at the door.

She soon pulled his arm and led him into the kitchen. "You hungry? Nothing fancy, but I just warmed up some soup and there's oyster crackers to go with it."

"I'm cool. I got something on the way over here. Are you okay? Do you want something more than soup? You know I can run out and get you something or I can order in for everybody. Is your mom and dad here?"

"I'm fine with this soup. They're here, but my mom is resting and my dad is in there with her."

"Okay. I'm worried about you though," he said, walking towards her as she ladled soup into a bowl. "I could tell you were crying on the phone, and don't take this the wrong way, but looking at you, it's obvious that you've been crying."

"I look that bad, huh?"

"No, no matter what, you always look good. I can just tell that you've been crying. About your son or Kim, too?"

"Yeah." She looked away from him.

He stood up from the table and walked over next to her and pulled her up to him, forcing her to look him in the eyes. "Renee, you know you can tell me anything, right? That little hesitation you just gave makes me think this is more than just about Kim or not meeting your son. Don't leave me in the dark, I'm here with you through it all."

Renee honestly believed that, but how could she tell any of them about Ted given how fragile those closest to her was. She didn't know what was going on with Pam, Monica and Keith's situation was taxing, and her mother and father took turns heavily grieving Kim's loss.

And Andrew, the way he had been so possessive and protective of her, if she told him, she didn't want to be the reason he went to jail if he sought out to hurt Ted.

She would tell them, but she knew it couldn't be now.

14

Darius

Given Monica's extraordinary ability to plan events from meetings for congressman to bar mitzvahs, it was nothing for her to get everyone to agree to come to her house for a much-needed game night. Had she not pulled it together, she would have spent another Friday night alone since Keith was still intent on ignoring her and the kids.

"So, how do you like being out there on the road, Mr. Funny Man?" Monica asked as she placed another bowl of chips on the table.

"It's alright," Darius said casually, not wanting the spotlight to be on him.

"Last night's show was off the chain, and I'm glad we had those first-row seats. I can't front, you were decent, but not as funny as I know you can be. Man up," Anthony said, laughing.

Darius gave Anthony a questioning look as if silently asking why he would bring that up in front of everyone.

"Don't mind them, Darius. I thought that you were hilarious."

"Thanks," he said giving Monica a half-smile.

"You've been moving around nonstop since we've been here, Monica. Tell me what to do and I can help you. Aye, where's Keith?" Darius looked at her.

"He's still at work. He's working on a tight deadline for a big project."

"I don't miss those times of punching someone else's clock as an accountant." He tried to grab the bowl from Monica's hands and help her, but she refused to let it go.

"No, that's okay. I'm the hostess. Just have a seat and enjoy yourself. Let's get these games underway." She plastered a smile on her face. "Okay, so let's get right to the best game of the night, taboo." She waved the box in the air. "Marcus, you and your wife will partner up. Vance, you and Pam. Renee, you and Andrew. Anthony, you and your wife." And whereas she would normally turn around and wink at Keith to confirm that they would be partners, she knew he wasn't mixed in the crowd.

A tear threatened to escape her eye, but she quickly fixed her face and looked over at Darius to pair him up. "And D—" She didn't even let the rest of his name leave her mouth because it would be a reminder that he would not be playing with Kim as he had so many other times.

Everyone looked at Monica who was looking at Darius, and of course, the rest of the sisterhood knew why she stopped mid thought. An eerie silence rested in the room.

"Well, looks like you and I will be partners, Darius," Monica said on a long breath.

Pam agreed to keep score and they decided to go in the order of length of relationships for each couple. Marcus and his wife went first, then Anthony and his.

They had made it through a few lackluster rounds of the game with no one saying what they knew a lot of the others were thinking—it was not as much fun as it normally was. They were missing Kim's quick-witted responses, the way she clowned everyone. The way her and Darius went back and forth with jokes made their game nights so much livelier than the current atmosphere.

"Okay Darius and Monica, it's y'all turn to go," Pam said.

Even as oblivious as Renee normally was to what was happening around her, even she could see that Darius and Monica's low score had nothing to do with them individually, but collectively. They didn't mesh well together.

If Kim had been alive and paired with Darius and if Keith were there with Monica, the competition between the two couples would've been fierce, relentless, with neither couple giving up until a tie breaking win declared the best duo for the night. The catastrophe of the mismatched pair in front of her was not what she witnessed during any of their other game nights.

Monica stood, brooding and tapping her foot, trying to get Darius to guess what word was at the top of the card.

It was a troubling sight.

He was hopeless in understanding her nonverbal cues because he felt she should've been using additional words to get him to guess the keyword on the card.

He and Kim had a system that worked perfectly. What he and Monica was doing, didn't.

"I'm sorry you guys, I can't do this anymore," Darius said and walked away from Monica.

The void of Kim not being there had become too much for Renee, not to mention her seeing Monica trying to hold it together in light of Keith not being there made her run out of the room. She didn't want to make a big scene with her tears.

"I'll go check on her," Andrew said.

"No, let us, please." Pam and Monica said in tandem as they got up and headed after Renee.

"We'll start cleaning up," Anthony's wife said and Marcus's wife nodded her head in agreement, leaving the men to themselves.

When they knew the women were out of earshot, they huddled around Darius.

"You alright, D?" Vance asked.

"No, man. I should have never come here."

"Nah, you did good coming here. We all haven't hung out together in a while," Anthony said.

"I saw you all last night at the comedy show and we've been keeping in touch with each other via texts," Darius said.

"But it's not the same, dude. We had come to do game nights often and we had real fun with everyone," Vance said. "And we haven't played ball together in like forever. It's time to put Andrew and Keith in the mix, too."

Marcus looked at Andrew. "And don't think that because you're a hot shot sports agent and represent some of the best basketball players in the league that we're chumps and you can beat us."

Andrew laughed.

"Yeah, we know that Kyle Irving is your boy and all, but we got game, too," Anthony said.

"Fellas, I didn't say y'all couldn't play." Andrew chuckled.

"We're just saying, so you know," Vance said. Everyone laughed. Even Darius cracked a smile.

"Leave the agent alone," Darius said. "I hear y'all reminiscing on what we used to do, but right now I'm on tour. I can't make any of that you're talking about happen." *Shoot, I need to focus on not getting kicked off the tour.*

Vance looked up at Darius and snapped his fingers. "Talking about what you used to do, I hate to say it D, but Anthony was right earlier. You just weren't your normal hit-em-non-stop joke telling self last night. You sure you okay?"

"I said I'm okay."

"We're your boys. You know you don't have to front with us and Andrew has been around long enough that I'm sure you can talk in front of him," Anthony said.

Andrew gave them a nod.

"I'm telling y'all I'm cool."

"D, think about how you were there for me and Vance when Pops was killed," Marcus said.

Darius let out a frustrated sigh and wiped his face. "I'm trying to do better. I went on the tour hoping that it would help me to get over all of this quicker. The first night I sucked big time, but the manager, knowing what I was going through and my real comedic talent, let me stay on the tour. I've been doing decent enough every night to stay on it, I think. But I guess being back here in Chicago really did something to me last night. It was my first time performing here since the funeral. She wasn't in the audience like I know she would've been if she'd still been alive.

"This is something that she would have wanted me to do. The fact that she's not here to celebrate it with me just pisses me off." He walked away from them and turned his back for a second before turning around again to face his lifelong friends. "I'm tired of feeling this way. It's like I get it together long enough to go on stage but then the other parts of the day, I'm sitting in the dark nursing a drink."

He saw the look of concern in their eyes. "Don't worry about that, I'm not an alcoholic. I sip on the same drink." He shook his head. "I just don't wanna be bothered with people."

"We're glad that you've opened up to us about this, but maybe you need to see someone," Marcus said.

"See someone?" Darius looked at them questioningly.

"Yeah, see a professional about your grief, like a grief counselor or a therapist or something," Marcus said.

"I'm black. I don't need a therapist. All I need to do is pray and I guess I'll get past this in time." Darius stared at them all.

"You don't really believe that, do you?" Marcus asked.

"You're damn right I do. I'll get over this. You of all people should know that the Bible says that earth has no sorrow that heaven can't heal."

"Yeah, but I also know that God gave wisdom to people like counselors and therapists to assist with issues we may have. Grief can be a hard thing to deal with and if you need to talk to somebody about it, then so be it. Going to see a therapist doesn't mean that you don't believe in God's healing power, it just means that you recognize all of the resources He's provided us to live our best lives," Marcus said.

"Shoot, I couldn't get it up the other night, I don't need a therapist, maybe a doctor, but not a therapist," Darius mumbled.

"What?" Anthony asked

"Nothing, man, nothing." He looked over at Marcus who was giving him a "take my advice" look. "Whatever, black men don't go see therapists. We either pray, tell jokes, or ignore our feelings. Tell the ladies I said good night, I gotta get out of here." He saluted them and headed towards the door.

"Wait." Anthony stood up and rushed to stop Darius's exit. "This may sound crazy to y'all, but if you're not willing to see a therapist, while it may be too soon to date again, maybe you should go out with a woman just for companionship or something."

"Come here so I can knock some sense upside your head," Vance said with his mouth slightly ajar, staring at Anthony.

"I'm serious. I didn't say fall in love or marry a woman. Just get a friend for companionship. If he won't talk to a therapist, maybe he'll open up to a female friend."

Darius could see that Marcus, Vance, and even Andrew were getting riled up to speak but he cut them off with the lift of his hand. "Don't worry, fellas. I'm not taking Anthony's advice to heart. Good night." He shook his head and headed for the door, this time, without protest.

Little did the fellas know that he'd tried Anthony's suggestion and failed. Although he didn't open up and talk to her about his feelings, he learned that his equipment below his belt didn't work anymore. To him, that meant a woman may not so easily help him deal with his grief.

15

Monica

"I can't believe you're as big as you are already," Pam said, staring at Monica.

"Hey, I'd expect Kim to say something like that to me, not you." She swatted at Pam.

The mention of Kim quieted them.

"Ladies, let's be honest with ourselves. We're gonna bring her up, probably for the rest of our lives. She played such an integral role in our sisterhood that it's hard not to talk about each other without somehow still including her. In fact, I think it's healthy to talk about her, remember the good times, rather than pretend like she didn't exist like some people I know do." Monica said the last of her words under her breath.

"Right, we don't want people always walking out of the room whenever she's mentioned. Let's lean on one another to continue to heal," Pam chimed in.

"You're right. It's just hard talking about her in the past tense," Renee uttered.

"I know, but we have to keep her spirit alive," Monica said, rubbing her belly.

"Okay, so Monica, it's your time to shine first," Pam said as she settled into the oversized chair near the fireplace.

Monica snarled. "Do I really have to go first?"

"Yes, you do." Pam smirked.

"Well," she adjusted on the couch, pulling her right leg from under and replacing it with her left before continuing, "not that I was avoiding sharing this with you, but since Renee stopped by right when she returned, I already told her that Keith has been...he's been—"

"He's been what?" Pam's voice elevated and her eyes widened as she stared directly at Monica.

"He's been emotionally and physically unavailable to me since Kim died." Monica cleared her throat. She desperately tried to wish away any signals that she might cry. She had been doing too much of it over the matter.

Pam got up from her chair and squeezed in between Renee and Monica on the oversized sofa. "I'm sorry, honey. I wish you would've told me sooner. I would've come over more often, helped out more with the twins."

"Thanks, but this is not on you. You call often and answer when I call to chat with you."

"So why didn't you tell me sooner? I thought we said no more secrets," Renee asked, pouting, but then fixed her face, remembering what she was keeping from them.

"Yeah, well, I didn't count this one as a secret, more like a marital issue. I know I have to be careful with what I say about my husband to others. If it's something negative, they'd still not like him long after we've made up."

"You're right, but can you hold that thought while I run to the bathroom real quick?" Pam's soft brown eyes stared right at Monica. "I'm serious, I really need to go to the bathroom, but don't want to miss any of this conversation." Pam stood and headed out the room.

"Really?" Monica said with her head cocked toward Pam's fleeting back.

"Really. I'll be right back," she shouted just before closing the half bathroom's door down the hall.

She was back with them and rejoined her seat in no time. "Okay, Like I was saying," she squeezed Monica's hand trying to recapture the sentimental and serious moment they were sharing before her bathroom break, "I don't need to know you alls personal business, I just don't want you to ever feel like you're alone in life because you and he are not on the best of terms. You know you'll always have us." Pam squeezed Monica's hand and then looked between her and Renee, who sat quietly near her.

"I know, and I love you all so much for always being shoulders to lean on. This is just a lot for me." She wiped at her tears. "I understand that he's still grieving, but so am I. He used to be so reassuring, my rock, but I haven't felt his touch, his strength since her death. I'm not narcissistic, but it scares me that he doesn't dote on me the way he used to. It makes me feel unwanted like I'm not enough for him anymore. Like I'll never be enough for him anymore. I just don't know how to get through to him." Monica's head dropped and she whimpered softly.

Fully alert now, Renee got up to sit on the opposite side of Monica and began rubbing her back. "You have to know that's not true. While Keith's behavior towards you is definitely uncharacteristic of him, I'm certain he's not so far gone to the point that he doesn't want you anymore, that he'll never want you again. You'll always be hot, pregnant or not. You know you're the apple of his eye."

"She's right, you know?" Pam said, patting Monica's arm.

"I'm not trying to make excuses for him, but we've never had to deal with the death of a close loved one, so I don't even have a reference point to say how he was before and that he'll come to grips with the reality of it all at a certain point. I wish I knew exactly what to tell you, but I don't. But I will tell you that I'll talk to him again." Renee said the last of her words with a Kim-like snip that widened both Monica and Pam's eyes. They both stared at her with raised eyebrows.

She looked at them. "What?" Sincere alert was in her voice.

Monica cleared her throat from her residual cries and said, "Had I not been looking at you when you just said that, I would've sworn Kim said it."

"Yeah, Renee, you sounded just like Kim, tone, voice, and sass," Pam added.

"You waited until she's gone to get that sass she was trying to pull out of you all along." Monica chuckled.

Renee shrunk back into the couch and folded her arms across her chest, pouting. "Not sass. I wasn't being sassy. It just needed to be said. Clearly, my brother needs a good talking to."

Monica and Pam looked at each other before toppling over in laughter.

"What? Renee asked, confused again.

"You're still acting like Kim. The dramatics of you pouting. At least we know you can pull on her strengths when needed."

"Yeah, my sissy was strong." Renee traced the box patterns of her flannel plaid shirt.

"She was, and you know she'd get you right now if she saw what you were wearing." Pam pulled on Renee's top.

"What?" Renee looked down at herself then back up with a scrunched forehead at her friends. "I don't have on a long jean skirt today, I have on jeggings." She stood up and twirled before splaying her hands out as if to say, "Look at me. Aren't I cute?"

"We see you, but can we pause the conversation again? I really have to go potty."

"Again? It wasn't that long ago when you just went," Monica whined.

"Hey, don't judge me. I'll be right back and once again, hold the conversation until I return." Pam shuffled down the hall, handled her business, and then came out of it to see Renee and Monica staring at her. "Hey, I'm getting something from the fridge real quick since I know you keep snacks, Monica. You ladies want me to grab you something?"

Monica looked incredulously at Renee.

Pam shrugged. "Suit yourselves." She rushed the refrigerator knowing Monica always kept fresh cut fruit in it. She grabbed a whole container of pineapples, bottled water, and cayenne pepper from a cabinet. She rushed back down the hall to see Renee seated again and sat back down next to Monica who was staring at her.

Renee leaned forward and openly stared at Pam as she sprinkled cayenne pepper on the pineapples and moaned as she bit into one.

Pam smacked her tongue against the roof of her mouth. "Delicious," she said to herself before looking over at her friends. "Okay, I'm back and yes, we applaud you for ditching the skirt today, but that plaid shirt of yours is long enough to constitute as a dress."

"So you focus the conversation on me, which you know I hate, but we should be discussing your snack choice right now," Renee said.

"We know you hate attention, but I need to be caught up on what happened with you while you were away. So yes, it's your turn to dish. That is, unless you have more to talk about, Monica." Pam looked to Monica. "And we've put cayenne pepper on pineapples before, no biggie now."

"No." Monica slowly raised a brow, staring at Pam savoring each pineapple chunk she covered with the red powder. "No, there's nothing more for me to say. I know we'll pray before y'all leave. Our prayers together always help. And we've never put cayenne pepper on pineapples, watermelon maybe, but not pineapples."

"Oh, but this is good. Wanna taste?" She held one out to Monica.

"Eww, that stinks. Don't make me throw up. Clearly, the babies don't like it." She rubbed her stomach and frowned at Pam.

"Sorry," Pam said, scooting over and putting distance between her and Monica. She closed her eyes and moaned as the sweet and spicy flavors blended into a beautiful medley in her mouth.

Renee shook her head. "We can pray now then. Come on, let's hold hands and bow our heads." She stood and motioned for their hands to join hers.

Monica grabbed her hand but pulled her back down to the couch. "We know you love to pray, and you're not off the hook with catching up Pam and I with what's new with you, but we'll have to table that for a second." She pushed Renee back flat against the couch to stare at Pam at the other end of the couch "What I really wanna know is, what's up with you, missy?"

Having just tipped the bowl of pineapples up to her mouth to drink the juice from it, she finally looked at them staring at her. "What?" she said, wiping her mouth with her sleeve and then guzzling down her bottle of water.

"Don't what me. You've rushed off to the bathroom twice within the last twenty minutes and just smashed that big bowel of pineapples covered in cayenne pepper. Something ain't right. Wait."

"What?" Renee asked, noting the shock and alarm in Monica's voice.

Ignoring Renee's normally aloof demeanor, Monica's eyes widened and she struggled a little to push herself up from the low couch. When her feet were finally flat on the floor, she made her way down to the end of the couch. Her eyes narrowed, her mouth tightened with merriment, and she pointed a finger at Pam. "Is there something you want to share with us?"

"No." Pam blurted out and jumped up to rush past Monica.

Monica laughed. "Oh no, you aren't getting away without answering my question."

"What question?" Renee asked, confused.

"I don't know what you're talking about, Mon. I'm gonna throw this stuff away and I have to go to the bathroom again."

Monica was close on Pam's heels, but Pam was faster than her and made it to the kitchen to discard her trash and in the bathroom before Monica could block its entrance as Pam figured she would try to do.

"What, I don't get it," Renee said, finally catching up to Monica outside of the bathroom.

Monica looked at Renee. "I love you, but I swear you can be so out of it sometimes."

"Out of what?"

Monica shook her head and crossed her arms across her middle. They eventually rested on her protruding stomach as one foot tapped on the floor. "So you can't connect the dots of her using the bathroom so frequently and eating that weird snack?"

"No."

They heard the toilet flush and water running on the other side of the door.

"Clearly you don't, but you will in a second."

There was silence on the other side of the bathroom door.

"We're not going anywhere so you might as well come out now and face the music." Monica smirked.

Renee's face marred with lines.

The door slowly opened and a nervous Pam stepped out into the hallway with her two best friends. Monica was perched on one wall and Renee slightly leaned against the other.

Pam clasped her hands in front of her and stared at the floor, biting the inside of her mouth.

"Really, Pam?" The humor in Monica's voice was loud and clear.

"What? You saw what I was eating and drinking, mainly water. If it goes in, it has to come out. Now let's pray so I can get home to my husband. We'll schedule another girls' night soon." Pam squared her shoulders and tried to walk off, but Monica shifted so that she stood centered in the hallway. Her arms stretched out wide to the sides of her provided no way for Pam to get past her.

Pam huffed. "You tell me what you think it is you know so I can shoot it down and then I can leave."

"We all are special." Monica laughed. "We know what each other's tell signs are and yet we still try to hide stuff from one another. For example, you're biting mighty hard on the inside of your jaw which means you're lying that nothing's going on with you. What are you keeping from us?"

Monica went closer to Pam and began to sniff her.

"Monica, why are you doing that?" With the high pitch in her voice and scrunched face, Renee left no room that she was still confused.

Monica sniffed Pam again. "You're pregnant, aren't you?"

"Sniffing me? What are you, a hound dog? Part of the K-9 unit for the police?" Pam said, feigning annoyance.

Monica laughed. "Don't try and deflect. You're pregnant, aren't you?"

Renee's eyes widened and so did her smile. She stepped closer to her friends. "Are you?" She looked directly at Pam.

Pam huffed. "No."

"You're lying. Biting the inside of your jaw again and avoiding making eye contact with us. You're lying. You are!" Monica squealed and clasped Pam's hands in hers as she jumped up and down hoping the other two would join in her celebration.

Renee's mouth was slightly ajar and looked as if she was holding her breath waiting for Pam's response.

Monica stopped jumping up and down, realizing neither one of her friends were celebrating with her.

"How far along are you?" Monica asked.

Pam bit harder into the inside of her jaw, but the excitement in her wandering eyes didn't go unnoticed by Monica.

Monica pulled her in for a tight embrace and pulled away only to squeal in delight. "I'm so happy for you, and even though I must be a lot farther along than you are, we'll still be pregnant together for a while. The twins will have their cousin as a playmate." She pulled Pam in the direction of the den they were in earlier, but she stopped and looked back at Pam with what she thought was an ingenious idea. "What if you're pregnant with twins like me?"

Renee appeared next to them. "But Monica, she didn't even say that she is pregnant. Don't you think you're jumping to conclusions?"

Monica shot a baffled look at her. "Renee…" She let her words trail off disappointed that Kim wasn't there to handle the sarcastic responses to Renee that only she could deliver so wittingly.

"Okay, so even if it's not twins, we're still pregnant together and our babies will be playmates. Oh, now I really hope that it's all girls so they can be a sisterhood like we are."

Pam knew that Monica would go on and on if she didn't stop her. She deadened her weight, forcing Monica to stop pulling her short of the step into the den. "Monica, I can't talk about this now…I haven't even told Vance." She hushed the last of her words. However, Monica heard her.

Monica looked back at her. "Why not? Is something wrong?"

"Not in the way you think, it's just—it just hasn't been the right time to tell him. Not with the—", she stopped herself. She couldn't bring up or even allude to his promotion that might send her out of state. With what Monica had going on with Keith, she needed to be there for her friend, and Renee hadn't connected with her son yet. She didn't want to leave her friends and she certainly didn't feel like it was the right time to tell them that there was even the possibility of her moving.

"Not with the what? What's going on, Pam?" Monica said, concern oozing from every part of her body as she inched closer to Pam, her eyes focusing even more so on her.

"It's nothing. Really, nothing." Trying to take the attention off of what she almost let slip, she said, "Yes, I'm pregnant."

Monica squealed and Renee finally smiled.

"It's not that I don't want you guys to know, I just think Vance was supposed to know before anyone else. Can you all please not tell anyone? I'll let you know when I tell him."

"Yay," Renee said and threw her arms around Pam. Monica joined in the group hug.

Monica soon pulled back. "I won't tell anyone, but you know this means our kids will have their own special bond. Oh, I am so looking forward to the cute playdates with them. And now I really hope you do have twins." Monica laughed as she moved out of reach of Pam's swatting hand.

They all embraced one another again.

Monica was happy that she had something to focus on other than her crumbling marriage. Not even knowing how far along Pam was, her event planning wheels were already spinning in how she could plan the best baby shower for her friend. She knew she'd have to make it over the top since Pam didn't have the traditional, walk-down-the-aisle wedding.

16

Darius

"Darius, this is the last night, brother."

Darius huffed and dropped his head as he leaned against the walls in the hallway.

Greg, manager of the comedy tour, continued on, "I've given you more chances than I should have at this point because I know how funny you really are. You're one of the ones that can go far in the biz. Get your own TV show one day, sell out arenas as a headliner, but that can't ever happen with the subpar performances you've been putting up."

Darius rubbed his face. His goatee and connecting beard making noise from the friction with his palms.

"Look, man." Greg stepped closer to him and laid one hand on Darius' shoulder. "I know losing your woman was a lot to deal with, but if you can't get it together, ASAP, like right now, I have to let you go. I mean, tonight's performance was just enough to give you one more try, but if you don't kill the night after tomorrow, I'll have to drop you from the tour and send you on your way. You're a cool, funny dude, but this is business. You understand?"

"Yeah, I do," Darius said low as he finally looked up to make eye contact with Greg.

"Good, I'm counting on you to get it together." Greg extended his hand and pulled Darius into a one-armed, brotherly hug.

He started down the short hall heading towards the stage but looked back at Darius. "Hey, talk to somebody, professional if you need to. This is a once in a lifetime opportunity. Don't let it pass you by without giving it all you've got." He nodded at Darius and then walked off.

Darius rubbed his face one last time and turned to head to the small dressing room he shared with two other comedians on the tour. He peeked in first to see if anyone was in there. Satisfied that he'd be alone, he stepped in and closed the door.

He was thirsty and stressed. He walked towards the makeshift bar preparing to grab his favored drink of choice since her passing, Hennessey, when he shook his head and mumbled, "I've been rocking with you but you ain't helping me deal with this." He grabbed the bottle of water next to it instead. He walked to the small leather sofa and fell back on it, adjusting as his black leather jacket rustled against the leather sofa.

"I don't wanna lose this opportunity. I have to get it together, but professional help? Talk to a shrink? That ain't my style. I just tell jokes and work through the minimal stress I used to have before she passed. This is all of your fault." He said the last of his words as if Kim was in front of him and could hear him.

"My life was good before you, even better with you, but now? Got me needing to see a head doctor." He quieted himself thinking he heard someone trying to enter the small space. After seconds of silence and no one opening the door, no sound outside of it, he resumed his conversation with himself. "Maybe I do need to talk to someone, hell, I guess it's better than talking to myself."

He pulled out his smart phone and opened the chrome app. The vertical thin line blinking called him to type something to direct its search. "Nothing beats a try." He typed in therapists in Chicago. Although he was on tour and would probably need someone mobile, or at least someone he could talk to on the phone if he needed to, Chicago was home and he could get back to it quicker than any other city.

He scanned the list of professionals. "Man or a woman? Forget a man, I can keep my money and just talk to my boys about it if that's the case. But can those knuckleheads really help me?" He chuckled.

"We've been tight since college. Yeah, they're each smart in their own rights, but I could see hardly getting anywhere with them in a convo between all of the clowning we'd do with one another. Wait, I'm the comedian. I'm the one mainly derailing our convos, lightening them up with humor. A woman would probably be better, but how can a woman tell a man how to think, how to feel, how to deal with his issues? Maybe I should just figure this out all on my own."

He stopped his monologue and focused his eyes on his new friend, the bottle of Hennessey. "Nah, you ain't helping me either." He eeny-meeny-miny-moed between the first five sites visible on his phone screen and clicked the link leading him to Danielle Wyndham's site. He mulled over one line, *I specialize in helping people cope and manage their grief.*

"My coping mechanisms aren't helping me and I'll manage to get kicked off this tour if I don't get right." Despite his reservations about talking to someone about his feelings, he pressed the link to dial the number to the therapist's office.

"Hello, you've reached the office of Dr. Danielle Wyndham. We're unable to answer your call now, but if you leave a brief message, we'll be sure to get back to you at our earliest convenience."

The phone beeped signaling him to leave his message.

He rushed through leaving a message. "Well, at least I gave it a try." He doubted they would get the message in the morning, get back to him, and give him enough time to get back to Chicago, but as fate would have it, he saw there was an option to schedule appointments online.

"Damn," he mumbled as he clicked on the calendar and chose the next available appointment which was that next day at 11:00 a.m. He opened up another window on his phone to see that there was an open flight back to Chicago at 6:00 a.m. He booked it first and then went back to the doctor's site to finish booking his appointment.

When finished, he dropped his phone on the side of him and braced his interlaced hands on his forehead. He sighed. "Alright Darius Tolliver, let's see if this head doctor can fix you."

***

Darius walked into the office suite located not too far from south Lake Shore Drive and took in the décor. Neutral colors. "They're going for soothing in here? I would think they would splatter bright colors everywhere, try to make people cheery upon entry," he mumbled to himself.

The receptionist's lips parted but said nothing as her eyes did a quick sweep of Darius from head to toe.

"May I help you?" She slowly licked her lips as she made direct eye contact with him.

Darius rubbed the base of his neck. "Um, I'm here to see Dr. Wyndham." He stuffed his hands in his pockets and looked around the office, to anywhere, but the receptionist still openly ogling him. He was never one to shy away from flirting with a woman, but his purpose for being there stunted any inkling he may have had to take on a new adventure with a woman.

His last run in with a woman, the one he took back to his hotel room, confirmed he wasn't ready to move on from Kim, hence his reason for being in that office.

"And you are? ...fine as ever." She hushed the last of her words hoping he didn't hear her.

He heard her and it stalled him from responding. He would readily admit that his above average height, full, muscular build, smooth, butterscotch skin, and strong, chiseled face put him on most women's radar. But her open appraisal of him was discomforting to him.

He wasn't ready to look back at her for fear of what else she might say or whatever salacious look she might give him.

Appearing to be in her mid-forties, and with her smooth, dark skin, full lips, and round shaped eyes, she wasn't a bad sight, but he just wasn't interested in what she seemed to want to offer him. He spoke up with his back still facing her, acting as if he was engrossed in a stack of pamphlets hanging on a wall rack. "I'm Darius Tolliver. I have an eleven o'clock appointment."

"Oh, so you're Darius. A handsome face to match the sexy voice from the voicemail left last night. In fact, you look even better than how you sounded."

He could've sworn he heard her moan and a slurping sound. That was the last straw for him.

He'd honestly had enough of her inappropriate behavior. Granted, he was a comedian, a stellar flirt, and could go back and forth with the best of them, considering himself amongst the greats, but being an accountant by profession, he was also a stickler on professionalism. He turned to face the receptionist ready to demand he speak to her superior to report her when Dr. Wyndham entered the reception area.

"Audrey, would you please—" she stepped out of her office with a long wool pea coat on and looked over to see Darius standing, fuming. Noting his rigid posture, but unsure of why, she looked back to her receptionist. "I was just going to tell you that I was going to run to the café a few doors over to grab my special before my eleven o'clock showed, but it looks like he's here already. She turned and walked towards Darius and extended her hand to him. "Hello, I'm Dr. Wyndham, and you must be Darius Tolliver?"

He accepted her outstretched hand and her warm smile and couldn't help but to calm his brooding attitude. "Yes. Pleasure to meet you, Dr. Wyndham."

She released his hand and looked back to Audrey. "Have you had him fill out his insurance info yet?"

"No, I was just getting ready to when you came out."

"Okay, well how about while you have him do that, I'll run over and grab my espresso?" Dr. Wyndham looked to Audrey.

"Yes." Audrey smirked.

"No," Darius said so adamantly that Dr. Wyndham snapped her neck in his direction and gazed at him with wary focus.

"No? Is everything okay?" You're here early," she looked down at her watch, "so we have fifteen minutes before your session begins."

Realizing his tone must've been too harsh, he took in a deep, hopefully, calming breath, and said, "I'm sorry, I just…" He looked at Audrey staring at him with a hint of mischief in her eyes before her face went stoic when Dr. Wyndham looked at her as well. "Never mind." He was no longer in the mood to raise hell over the receptionist's antics.

In fact, he was no longer in the mood to do the session. "You know what? I think I need to reschedule this. Is there a fee to cancel so late?"

Dr. Wyndham briefly studied Darius. His eyes were trained on her and she could see the exhaustion in them. Knowing that grieving patients often avoided the measures that would start their healing journey, she refused to let him leave without talking to him.

She grabbed the clipboard from Audrey. "How about you follow me in my office and we can fill it out together." She turned to Audrey. "Can you please be a dear and run and get my drink order? I promise I'll bring in a new Keurig tomorrow. Thank you," she said to Audrey over her shoulder as she motioned for Darius to walk ahead of her.

Being the gentleman that he was, he held the office door open for her until she crossed the threshold.

"Please, take a seat on the couch or at the chair in front of my desk, whichever one you'd prefer."

Not wanting it to feel like an all-out shrink session, he opted to sit in the chair at her desk.

She rounded her desk, handed him the clipboard she held, then sat in her comfy leather seat. She watched him studying the questionnaire she'd given him.

"Just fill out the insurance info and I'll have Audrey fill out the rest and process it while you're in here with me." She gave him some time to do as instructed before she said, "So, Mr. Tolliver or can I call you Darius?"

"Darius is fine." He looked up at her after placing the clipboard on her desk.

"How are you today?"

"I'm as good as any other day." He sat back in the seat and clasped his hands across his stomach.

"And how is that?"

"I don't know, just decent."

"Okay." She reached for her legal pad on her desk.

She picked up an engraved pen and tapped against her smooth caramel chin as she looked back at him. "If you wouldn't mind elaborating, what's decent for you?"

"Look, Dr. Wyndham," he scooted to the edge of his chair, "I set up the appointment because I needed to do something to keep this once in probably a lifetime opportunity I have. See, I'm a comedian, really an accountant, but I'm trying my hand at being a comedian. I'm on the Laugh Out Loud tour."

She nodded at him.

"I'm one of the funniest men you'll probably ever meet. Problem is, that Darius Tolliver hasn't shown up to the tour yet."

"Which leads you here, right?"

He nodded slowly.

"I was trying not to dive straight into it, but who passed?" she asked.

"You know what, like I was saying, I came her in hopes of trying to figure out how to put my head full of jokes back on stage, but I can't do this. I can't open up to a complete stranger. I'll just figure this out on my own." He stood to leave. "Sorry to waste your time."

All five feet and eight inches of her solid 160-pound frame stood up with him. "Wait, Darius."

Her calming voice halted his steps. He turned to look back at her.

"There was something, external and internal, that pushed you to seek out help. Just try it out."

He looked at her and opened his mouth to protest, but she silenced him by holding up her hand and saying, "How about this session is on me. Here, you come over and sit on the couch." She walked near it and motioned for him to sit. "Why don't we just sit over here and chat a little while longer."

He stared at her for a beat before he accepted her offer to sit.

When she was satisfied that his slumped body against the couch might not dart out of the door, she took a seat in the chair opposite him.

"I know you think of me as a stranger and that's fair because technically, I am. Even though some people have great support systems around them, they're still hesitant to confide in those people in certain situations. If that's your case, I may be the perfect sounding board for you. Just give it a try." She smiled.

He just stared at her. "I shouldn't even be here."

"Why not?"

"Because, I'm a man. I'm supposed to be strong, right? Never let anything get to me. And I'm black on top of that." He sat up, leaning in to say, "You know we don't do therapy, we just pray and keep it moving." He cracked a smile, but she didn't. "Okay," he mumbled under his breath and sat back again. "I guess I'm not that funny to you," he said loud enough to be heard.

"No, I can imagine you are, but forgive me if I can't make light of or find the humor in the two fallacies you just stated."

He raised one eyebrow at her.

"For one, although it may have been erroneously passed down from older generations that men are supposed to be strong, never cry, never let anyone see them sweat, and things of that nature, research and if I can be quite frank with you," she didn't wait for him to give her permission, she just continued on saying, "good common sense says that is just plain wrong."

He cleared his throat and shifted in his seat.

She smoothed out her heather gray pencil skirt and took a quick deep breath to remain neutral and professional as she worked to dispel the myths she just learned that Darius was armed with about proper mental health. "You're human. You're not meant to shoulder life, the good and the bad, alone. And to think that you're supposed to will only hinder you from experiencing your best life."

He folded his arms across his chest and stretched his legs out in front of him, crossing his ankles.

She had to keep from cocking her head prior to her next words. "And the idea that black people shouldn't seek out professional help in the form of therapists and the likes and just simply pray is wrong. Off the record?" She looked to him to accept her offer.

He nodded and she continued. "You won't find it in a medical book, but I'd like to think that God empowers therapists, psychologists, and counselors with the knowledge and wherewithal to reach and help people in the ways we do." She leaned in. "And FYI, what really makes you a strong black man is your willingness to admit that you can't get through this season in your life on your own and that you are strong enough to seek out help to improve your mental state. So no, I don't think it's weak and wrong of you to be sitting here looking to better cope with the loss of a loved one."

He stiffened in his seat.

"Darius, remember, I specialize in grief counseling, there's not much else you would be here for."

Sighing, he mumbled, "My girlfriend."

"Okay, your girlfriend. Was it sudden or did you all know it was coming? How long has it been since she passed?"

Still reluctant to discuss Kim with anyone, he refused to make eye contact with her as he finally answered the question. "It was sudden to me and she passed months ago."

"Okay and how long had you two been together?"

"Well, see…"

Dr. Wyndham eyed him cautiously.

"See, I considered us to be in a relationship towards the end, before that, I was just having fun with her for about two years."

"Okay. Did she feel the same way about you as you did about her?"

Darius sat up some, resting his forearms on his knees. "I'd like to think so." He looked down, clasping his big hands before he looked back up at her. "Yeah, she did, she was just too afraid to show it."

"Good to know." Dr. Wyndham left her chair long enough to grab the legal pad and pen from her desk.

"Start wherever you want, tell me as much as you'd like, I think the more you talk, the beneficial it will be for you."

Darius took a deep breath and released it staring at her bearing such a calming presence. *I'm here. I might as well use my time wisely.* "It all began about two years ago when I met her at my friend Vance's elementary school. He was the principal and was throwing a barbecue for his staff…"

Twenty-nine minutes later, Darius had given her an abbreviated, yet thorough recap of his time with Kim and up until what he did the day before.

"Well, of the five stages of grief, and not to say they can always be perfectly separated, it sounds like you're in the stage of depression."

"I'm not depressed. I don't have suicidal thoughts." Darius raised his voice.

She took a visibly deep breath in hopes that he would mimic the gesture and return to a more docile demeanor. "Depression doesn't always manifest itself in suicidal thoughts, activities, and attempts. It can appear as overeating, not eating at all, fatigue, poor concentration, and things like that. If you're sad all the time, merely coasting through life, and in your case, you're in a grief-induced state of depression, Darius."

"Okay, so how do I get out of it then?"

"I'm glad you asked." She offered him a genuine smile. "You said you're on a comedy tour, right?"

"Yeah."

"But on the verge of being kicked off?"

"Yup." He sighed.

"Why?"

"Because I'm not bringing that electric, heart racing, stomach clutching humor to the stage I normally do."

"Why do you think that's the case?'

He opened his mouth to speak, but nothing came out. He looked at her for a moment contemplating if it were really okay of him to say the first thing that came to his mind.

Her relaxed posture and soft features made him say, "I guess I haven't been the same since she passed. I agreed to do the tour thinking it would give me the boost I needed to get past losing her, but it just isn't doing that. It's like I'm just putting up a grand enough façade to make it through my sets."

She jotted something down on her legal pad and then looked back up at him. "Okay, some great ways to overcome depression are to partake in social activities and stay connected to people. I'd say the comedy tour is your social activity at the moment, but it doesn't seem to be doing what you need or hoped it would do. Are there any other activities you enjoy?"

Darius knew he couldn't say the first thing that came to his mind which was sex, and honestly, he'd only been interested in doing it with the person he was now grieving over. The safest thing for him to say was, "Basketball."

"Good. Have you played since she passed?"

"No, I went right on the tour a week after she passed. My days are spent performing at night and riding on the bus to the next tour city for the most part."

"And when is the tour over?"

"It may be over soon for me, but it doesn't officially end for another two months last time I checked. Everyone else has been doing so good with the overall show that we keep picking up new cities and venues to the tail end of it."

"It doesn't have to be over for you though. Remember I said another way to overcome depression is to stay connected to people. You may think you'd be a burden talking to others about how you feel, but I'm certain they wouldn't feel the same. Have you become buddies with any of the other comedians on the tour?"

"Nah, I keep to myself."

She jotted something else down on her pad. "Do you have any close friends that you can talk to?"

"Yeah, my best friends, more like brothers, Anthony, Vance, and Marcus."

"Have you talked to them at all about how you feel over losing her?"

"A little, but I didn't really open up to them, so they encouraged me to speak to a professional like yourself."

"That's good that you have friends that were trying to help you and when they realized they couldn't, they encouraged you to seek it out elsewhere. From what I've gathered thus far, you have social activities you enjoy and could engage in if you tried them to help your grief. You also have people to help keep you from being depressed, you just haven't accessed them the way you could.

"The reality is, with her death not being so long ago, you're within your rights to still feel some type of helplessness, anger, sadness, despair, but the goal has to be to not dwell in those feelings. You can't allow them to cripple you."

He nodded.

"You expressed your apprehensions about talking to me at first, but are you feeling more at ease with talking about your feelings, when you're sad about her, with me? Your friends?"

"I'm more open to talking to you about it all now."

"Great." She gave him a toothy smile and then looked at her watch. "Well, it's been an hour. I would love to continue with you today, but I have a 12:15 appointment." She stood up and re-buttoned her fitted, crimson blazer. She smoothed her hands over curvy hips, straightening out her skirt as she looked at him and said, "These sessions should be more of you talking than me talking. Sorry about that."

"No problem. Had you not said some of the things you said, I may not have said much at all."

She offered him another genuine smile. "And like I said, today's session is free, but to continue on, you can discuss with Audrey whether or not you'll be paying out of pocket or with insurance."

He grunted.

She squinted. "Is everything okay?"

"Yeah, it's just that your assistant was too flirty with me and I wasn't comfortable with it."

"I'm so sorry, Darius, I'll speak to her about it immediately."

"That's okay. I don't necessarily want to get her in trouble or anything, but you asked me a question and I figured the only way I can really make this thing work with you is, to be honest."

"Yes, honesty is the best policy. Don't worry about seeing Audrey on your way out. I saw that you filled out the form in its entirety, I'll give it to her." She walked over to her desk and grabbed a business card from it and then walked back over to hand it to him. "Here, take my card. It has the office number and my cell number on it as well. Since you're on tour and won't be in town much, call me when you need to. If I can't answer right then, leave a message and I'll get back to you as soon as I can. I don't want you feeling like you have to keep anything inside waiting until you see me again. Okay with that?" She looked him directly in his dark brown eyes.

"Sure." He offered her a half smile as he pulled the card from her grasp. "Thanks, Dr. Wyndham. Take care."

He turned to walk out but stopped when he heard her say, "Darius, there was too much finality in that 'take care' of yours. Please, call me whenever you need to."

"I will." He chuckled, finding something humorous for the first time that day. "Talk to you soon," he said with a hint of mirth lining his voice.

"Looking forward to it," she mumbled as the door closed behind him.

When she was certain he was out of earshot, she released a breath she had been holding on to since she first stumbled across him in her waiting room over an hour ago.

Sad and definitely unprofessional to admit to another soul, she understood why Audrey must have been fawning over him. She couldn't imagine any sane woman who wouldn't, at the least, mentally salivate over his tall stature, well-conditioned girth of a basketball player, well-groomed appearance, full lips, and those slanted expressive eyes of his. And the one time he gave her an open mouth smile showing his perfectly aligned teeth, the act almost short-circuited her being.

Never before had she been so attracted to one of her male patients. She prided herself on her ability to keep her professionalism in tact at all times and although looking back, she thought she did a good job of disguising any and all traces of her instant attraction to him. She wondered if she really had.

After moments of mulling over the last hour with Darius and making her way back over to the chair behind her desk, she was satisfied that she had remained neutral with him.

But what was it about him that caught her attention in that way? She knew it wasn't wise for a professional provider to date a patient, let alone one who was grieving over a recently deceased partner, yet there she sat recalling every feature of Darius's she observed while he sat in front of her.

Granted she was supposed to observe him to assess his verbal and nonverbal cues as they talked, but Darius' handsome features and quiet charisma piqued her interest and her female anatomy in not so professional ways.

For the first time in twelve years of her counseling career, she questioned whether or not it would really be wise of her to continue her professional relationship with a patient when she'd much rather explore a more personal one with him.

She shook her head and her black, blunt bob swished against her chin before she smoothed the hairs back into place. She stood up and grabbed his chart from her desk and made her way to her office's door. She held on to the knob reminding herself that nothing could come of doting over a grieving man. She was the professional counselor and he was her patient. That's the only relationship that would ever exist between them.

17

Renee

"Enjoy your evening." Renee smiled at her coworkers on her way out the door.

She made it to her car, started it, and her head fell back against the headrest, letting out a long sigh. She was exhausted.

She had been back home for a little under two months and she was nowhere near catching up with the paperwork and cases that had piled up on her desk while she was away for that month in D.C. She guessed it was a good thing that she had so much work to do; it helped her not focus as much on still not being able to convince her son to meet her. And of course, it left minimal time for her to get sad about Kim no longer being around.

Although she wasn't grieving over Kim the way some may have thought she would've, she was getting grief from Andrew for them not spending enough time together. He understood her work entailed a lot of hours dedicated to it, but with his job keeping him out of town often, he wanted to spend every moment with her when he was home. It didn't always work out that way though.

It's not that she didn't want to be with him more often, that was the contrary. She knew she wanted him as a permanent fixture in her life, but now there was just too much going on for her to be as fully invested in them as she could be.

She was tired and would have loved to go home and go to sleep, but checking in with Monica earlier that day, she found out that yet another week had passed and Keith was still being cold and distant with her. They chided her for acting like Kim in recent times, but if that's what she needed to do to get through to him, she would. She could always apologize to him later if she was too harsh. Something Kim would never do.

Is he there? She hit Send, sending the text to Monica.

A beat passed before her phone vibrated. With her phone still in her hand, she quickly looked at the reply. *Yeah. He just came in, barely spoke to me or the kids and went straight to his office.* A crying emoji was placed at the end of her text.

Omw. Renee typed and hit Send. She buckled her seatbelt and pulled off, en route to Keith and Monica's.

Forty minutes later, she pulled up to their house. By the time she made it to the door, Monica had it open, waiting to embrace her.

Renee wrapped her arms around her sister-in-law, her best friend, and braced herself as Monica's weight rested on her. She couldn't see her face, but she knew she was crying, given her heaving shoulders and the soft sobs in her ear.

She slowly rubbed Monica's back and said, "I'm sorry, Mon. Let me go talk to him and I'll be back out to check on you and the babies." Renee gave Monica one last squeeze before she exited their embrace and made her way to Keith's office.

She knocked, but no answer. "Keith, open the door." When she didn't hear a response or movement, she twisted the knob, but the door was locked. "Keith, let me in." She screamed and pounded on the door at the same time.

There was a shuffle behind the door and then it was snatched open allowing her to see a tight mouth and beady eyes staring down at her. "Stop screaming, you'll alarm the twins."

"Like you care," she said and pushed the door in, walking past him.

"What do you mean I don't care?" he said, closing the door behind him and turning a hard stare at her. "They're my kids. Of course, I care about them."

"According to Monica, you're still not paying her or them any attention."

He dropped his head.

Seeing the defeat written all over him, her Kim-like persona she was ready to enact deflated. "Keith." She stepped up to him and grabbed his hands in hers as best as she could, given his were much larger. "Keith," she threw her arms around his waist, "you've got to stop going on like this." Her voice was muffled against his chest.

His arms remained limp at his sides. It had been months since he'd gotten that physically close to someone. In fact, the last time he really hugged his sister, the only one he had left, was when he pulled her out of the hospital room after Kim stopped breathing. The memory rushing back to him made him grip Renee's arms and try to push her off him, but her hold on him was too strong.

After a bit more of a tussle, he finally stopped trying to fight her off. Her chest began to heave against his stomach and the instinct to protect her kicked in. He held her tightly as she cried against him.

"Keith, I miss her too. So much."

He said nothing.

"I guess I've been avoiding the pain of her loss by burying myself in reuniting with my son and getting back into the swing of things at work." She pulled back from him to look up at him. "And you, you're avoiding those you should be clinging to the most." She punched him as hard as she could in his chest and then hugged him one last time before she pulled away from him.

He kept his head low as he rubbed the spot she hit.

"You alright?" she asked, alarm in her voice and worried that she may have actually hurt her brother.

"Renee, it's not like you could really hurt me. You never could throw a punch. Now if Kim would've done it, it would've stung. She could pack a vicious punch. She wasn't just all mouth, she was just as much action." He chuckled before he covered his face and fell back against the door. He muffled his cry with hands as he slid down the wall, dropping to the base of it. She watched his shoulders jerk for quite some time and heard his sniffles as if he were trying to inhale his tears, his emotions, before she fell to her knees in front of him and hugged him as best as she could.

"Keith, talk to me." Her tears clouded her vision and her voice cracked. It had been a while since she cried, but seeing her brother had quickly opened the dam that had been guarding her tears.

"No, I'm supposed to be strong for you."

"It doesn't always work like that. You won't always be as strong as you want to. You need a shoulder, an ear right now and I'm here. Talk to me."

She sat with her legs folded in front of her and grabbed his hand. She squeezed it, urging him to talk.

He kept his head low and said, "This is the hardest thing I've ever had to do. I don't talk about her because I feel like I might break. So I keep my distance from Monica because she'll want to talk. And I just can't. I can't break down in front of my wife and kids. And Kalia," he huffed, "she looks so much like Kim I can barely look at her without wanting to bawl my eyes out. The least I can do is to keep it together enough to go to work and to continue to provide for them."

"To provide for them? Keith, you know what you need to provide the most for Monica right now?"

He didn't answer.

"Your love and support. The way you love her. That's what she needs right now. Don't you think she misses the special connection you all had? She learned you all were having twins on her own. What kind of support is that for her? She's getting bigger by the day and so are the twins. They need you. So do I." The unusual tremor in her voice made his head shoot up and look directly into her eyes.

She could see his wheels turning and hurried to speak to redirect his attention back on himself. "Keith, you've always been business savvy, so I know you have enough money set aside to take a leave of absence from work if you need to and deal with your grief in a better way."

He dropped his head again. "She doesn't even bother trying to talk much anymore. I think I've messed things up with her, long-term."

Renee could only rub his arm until his last sniffle and he looked up at her again.

"You haven't. That's why it hurts her so much, because she cares. She loves you so much."

"Look at you." He patted her face. "Here trying to get me right when I'm supposed to be the strong one for you." His eyebrows furrowed. "I heard something in your voice a second ago. Is everything okay?"

"Yeah…" She stalled before saying the last of her words. "Of course."

He eyed her a bit longer. "You sure? Because if it's Andrew, I can set him straight real quick. You promised to tell me if any dude ever tried to put his hands on you, remember?"

"Yeah."

"I'm not playing, Renee. I don't care how much you like him. How good of a guy he appears to be. I'm not letting another Ted happen to you." He clenched his teeth and she could see the strained veins in his neck.

She stiffened at the mention of that name. *Should I tell him now while we're on the subject? Nah, given how fragile he clearly is right now, that might drive him to do something he'll regret and possibly be separated from his family for a long time, if not for life.*

"Renee, is there something you're not telling me? I know I haven't been at my best these past months, but I promised to always be the brother you need me to be. You're the only sister I have left." A tear streaked his face as he dropped his head.

She reached out and grabbed his hand again. "I promise you that Andrew has been nothing but a gentleman to me. He's the best. There's nothing wrong between he and I. I know you'll always be here for me when I need you, but you made a vow to Monica, too. You're in covenant with her.

"Keith, you gotta deal with your grief and make things right with your family." She leaned forward and kissed him on his cheek before getting up and opening the door. She looked back one last time and said. "Make things right. Sooner than later. I love you."

He looked at her with pitiful eyes. She gave him a half smile and then walked out the door.

He finally stood up and closed the door, leaning his head against it. He mumbled to himself, "Yeah, I have to make things right sooner than later because later is not always promised. Lord, help me. Show me what to do."

18

Darius

"Hello."

"Hi, Darius."

"Dr. Wyndham," he said in a sing song voice. "How are you?"

"I'm great. I would ask how you are but given I can almost see that smile of yours through the phone from the way you just sang my name, I take it you're in good spirits?"

"Most definitely."

"I believe you. I saw a video someone posted of your set last night."

"Damn bootleggers," Darius griped. "Sorry, but they make the announcement before every show not to record knowing we'll be selling a mastered copy of the show when we do it at Madison Square Garden in New York, but people still wanna bootleg our hard work. Vultures."

"I know that cuts into you alls profits and bootlegging is wrong all together, but a plus of it is, more people are getting to know who you are."

"Yeah, I guess, but it still ain't right."

"I know, but by the time I was alerted of the video, it had reached a million views already."

Darius smiled.

"And the comments. Do you read them? The people on the thread of the video I watched raved about you and tagged their friends to see if they should get tickets when the tour comes to their city. One guy even said you should be headlining rather than one of the others."

"You know, what can I say?" Darius said, mimicking the famous line said by J.J. Evans on the 70s sitcom, *Good Times*.

Danielle found herself laughing.

"And what about you? Did you think I was funny?" Darius asked, shifting in his hotel bed.

She cleared her throat. Of course, she thought he was funny. And fine. She had saved all of the videos of him and laughed to the point of tears streaming her face with each video she watched.

Darius was insanely funny to her.

The charisma she knew he tamed during their first meeting in her office filled the stage, the venue, as much as the audience's laughter did from his jokes. She loved the up-close videos posted of him. It was like she had a front row seat to take in his broad shoulders, smooth butterscotch skin, and that mesmerizing smile of his.

She had never seen a man with a more brilliant, downright sexy smile than the one Darius bore when he talked. But she couldn't say any of that to him. It would seem so, so, fannish of her. Hot from thinking about him and hearing his deep, sexy voice on the phone yet again, she threw her throw cover off her. He spiked her temperature.

"Paging Dr. Wyndham. Are you still on call?" Darius asked.

"Hunh? Oh yeah, I'm still here."

"Good. So, do you think I'm funny?"

"You are." Her eyes darted from side to side gauging if her answer had come off neutral. They had been talking on the phone and video chatting so often since she started counseling him that she lost count of how many times she had to stop herself from flirting with him, telling him how sexy he was.

"Whew." He over exaggerated the word. "You know I have you to thank for giving me my mojo back when it comes to this comedy thing. If it weren't for you answering my many calls, no matter the time of day, encouraging me to work through some other things I didn't even know had shaped me over the years, I don't think I'd still be on the tour. You've kinda become my lucky charm, that's why I almost feel like I have to talk to you before I go on stage."

"Darius, you've thanked me plenty of times before, but as I keep telling you, it's not me, it's you. You're the one that's being honest and open about your feelings when we talk and employing the exercises I give you to ensure you're taking her loss in the right strides."

"You've made this all so much better and easier for me to cope. I was only existing after she died, but I kinda feel like I'll be able to live again. One day."

"You will." She smiled.

"So how much do I owe on your phone bill?"

"What?" She laughed.

"All the minutes I've used on it since I first came to your office."

"Darius, you know most carriers offer unlimited talk, text, and data nowadays."

"Right. I was just being silly. My mind drifted back to the days when people didn't talk much until after seven p.m. on the weekdays and all day long on Saturdays and Sundays."

The remembrance and just imagining him delivering the joke on stage garnered a hearty laugh from her.

"Glad to know I can make you laugh like that, doc." Darius popped the imaginary collar he had on given he was wearing a white tank top.

She was annoyed that the nature of their relationship kept her from telling him what else he gladly could make her do. She ignored her far from professional line of thinking and said to him, "Since you called me, I take it you have a show tonight?"

"You got it. I'll be getting up to get dressed pretty soon."

"Okay, so is there anything specific you wanted to discuss today?" Danielle asked, sitting up straight, hoping to emit her clinical credentials and not the school girl crush aura she normally quieted when talking to him.

Ugh, Ugh." Darius sat up on the bed and rubbed his closely cropped hair.

"Darius, you should know by now that whatever you share with me is safe."

"I do, but with this, you might judge me on it."

"No, I won't." She hated the accusation.

"Trust me, you might look at me differently if I share it with you and plus, I know you're my counselor, but I've come to see you as a friend, too."

The flat way he said "friend" stung her.

"I hadn't told the fellas because I knew they'd clown me on it. I didn't want to go see yet another doctor about it because I don't need the whole medical community in my business," he chuckled, "and telling you, a woman, this may ruin my rep with ladies in the future."

"Darius, you know doctor-patient privilege applies with our talks. I would never jeopardize my reputation by spilling your beans, nor would I betray your trust by telling your business."

"But friends break rules all of the time, don't they?"

There he goes throwing around that word 'friend' again.

She adjusted on the couch yet again. "I'm glad you consider me a friend, but doctor-patient privilege trumps all. I'm billing you for this conversation. Doctor-patient privilege applies."

"Ouch, doc. You're the most expensive friend I have." Darius laughed.

Danielle didn't.

"We should really discuss it if it will keep you on the right track with counteracting your grief."

"See, that's the thing, it's only ever happened to me once and I'm not sure if it's directly related to losing Kim or not." Darius rubbed his faced, questioning whether or not he should actually share his concern with her.

"Let's just talk through it and see if it's related."

"Okay, here goes... A few weeks after Kim passed, a fan, a beautiful one, one that looked like Kim, to be honest, approached me. One thing led to another and we were back at my hotel and she was all over me. She was about to, you know." He tilted his head to the side as if she could see him and read his facial expression.

"I know what, Darius?"

"You know."

"I don't. Just say it." She smoothed her hair down and took a deep breath to calm herself from wondering what the hussy from Darius' story was trying to do to him.

"I was trying to be couth with a lady like yourself,"

A lady like myself? What does he think, that I'm a prude? Some stuffy, buttoned up lady? Danielle finally tuned back in to hear him say, "but she was trying to give me some head, slob the knob, lick the—"

"Okay, okay, okay, I get your point." She held her hand up as if he could see her motion stopping him from using any other analogies to describe what the woman was trying to do. She cleared her throat. The subject matter wasn't lost on her, but for it to be the topic of conversation with Darius, him describing an intimate moment with another woman, oddly annoyed her. *Am I jealous? Wait, this is my patient, not my man.* So what was the problem?

"Do I have to say it?"

"You don't if you don't want to but if you don't, I'll never know if I can help you get through it."

"I couldn't get it up." Darius pulled the phone away from his ear, not ready to hear her cackle so closely in it. When he didn't hear laughter coming through the phone, he put it back up to his ear. "You still there, doc?"

"Yes. Why wouldn't I be?"

"I don't know, I thought maybe you or any woman for that matter, would turn their nose up at me, frown down on me, fall out of your chair laughing, knowing that I can't get it up."

"Couldn't or can't?"

"What do you mean?"

"I mean, was that just a one-time occurrence or has that been happening a lot lately?" She braced herself for whatever he was about to say, mainly how many women he'd been with because certainly a man that looked, talked, walked, and acted like Darius could bed as many women as he wanted to. And although he didn't give off the air that he was in a relationship or seeing multiple women, he was a man who had physical needs she was sure he was getting satisfied on the regular. Probably even while battling his depression.

"Doc, I haven't been with anyone since Kim. I didn't even really want to be with that woman that night, but I thought that maybe if I did, I could pretend like she was Kim and relive a moment with her or better yet, get over Kim quicker. I was just hoping to get out of my funk, suspend my grief, if nothing but for that night."

She let out a short yet relieved breath to know that he wasn't with a woman, even though she knew she could never be with him.

"So do you see my problem, what I'm nervous about? I've never not been able to perform and for that to happen, I wonder if it's permanently broke."

She covered her bow shaped mouth trying to contain her laughter. Hearing the honest worry in his voice over the matter really made her laugh, even if she wasn't supposed to.

"Dr. Wyndham, are you laughing at me?"

She sat up straighter and cleared her throat. "No, I'm not."

"Yes, you are. This is why I've never said anything to you, to anyone, about it."

"Darius, I promise I wasn't laughing at your issue, I was laughing at the alarm in your voice to think it's a permanent situation. I'm no M.D., but using my background knowledge, I'd say that you not being able to perform that night was all psychological. You've been healthily working through the stages of grief and doing well in my opinion since you started seeing me."

"I think so, too."

"If you're really that worried about it, you know there are ways to confirm or deny if it's still an issue."

"How so?" Darius's brain was strictly in professional help mode.

"Really, Darius? Do I have to spell it out for you?"

"Yes. What doctor can you recommend to go to for the tests?"

"No doctor needed." She smirked. "You can either do a test yourself or you can get a partner to help you figure it out."

Darius' face scrunched in wonder before it finally dawned on him her options to allay his fears. "So you're really telling me to do a mic check with my own hands or find some random woman to see if I can get it up with?"

"Yes, to the first one and not a random one. I'm certain you have known ones to choose from."

"Not down with the first one, I left that alone in high school. And Doc, I don't have a harem of women if that's what you're thinking. Like I said, I haven't been with one since Kim. Not that I was a dog before her, but I wasn't the relationship type and I did have a small rotation of women, but all of that changed with Kim. I became a one-woman man and if and when I do get back to dating, I think I'll keep that philosophy. She changed me."

"So you really haven't dated since Kim passed?" She asked more so for herself than for her anecdotes.

"Don't tell me that after all of this time getting to know me, you see me as some man whore?"

She caught herself from laughing unrestrained in his ear, like how she did when she watched his comedy clips. Her high-pitched laugh when something was too funny to her always included a snort. She couldn't imagine it would be sexy to him. She palmed herself in the forehead at the thought. *I'm not supposed to be worried about whether or not I'm sexy to him.*

"You still there or are you silent because you think so and don't want to flat out say it to me? I can take it straight, no chaser."

She cleared her throat, "Well, Darius, we've only discussed things related to your feelings about losing Kim, but I guess it's time to discuss what may be next for you in the love department. You said *if* you start dating again. Have you sworn it off for the time being, or are you really considering never falling in love again?"

Again, she found herself holding her breath waiting for an answer from him. As if his answer would reveal how he felt about her.

Darius shifted in his bed and rubbed his face, processing the question. A "no" was at the tip of his tongue, but he thought to weigh the question more. "Truthfully?"

"Yes, honesty is always the best policy."

"Of course, I wanna say I'll never date, love, again. Who signs up to possibly hurt themselves over and over? I don't think there will ever be another woman like Kim. So right now I can't see me falling for someone else, but with Kim, I learned the uncertainty of what the future holds. Get what I'm saying?"

"I guess." She heard her sarcastic tone before the words barely left her mouth and hated how she silently came undone, unprofessional when it came to Darius. She just hoped her tone was lost on him as it had been countless time before.

"Good."

"So if you really want to know if your erectile dysfunction was—"

"Whoa, whoa, whoa, let's not give it a name, Doc," Darius said hastily, jumping out the bed.

She laughed. "Well, that's what occurred but okay. In order to find out if your *dilemma* was situational or is an ongoing thing, you know the options to find out."

"You know what, Doc, I gotta go, this conversation..." he rubbed his head as he made his way to the bathroom.

"Darius, we're both adults. The subject matter isn't inappropriate for us, especially considering the nature of our interactions."

"I know all that, Doc, but I don't need you out here thinking I can't put it down, that I can't handle my business in the bedroom because I can. I puts it down."

With the way he dragged out the word down, Danielle had to close her eyes and take a long, calming breath. She'd love to be the recipient of him putting it down on her. *Focus, Danielle, focus.* "Darius, that's neither here nor there, but what is relevant is you knowing that it's okay to try love again when you're ready. It's okay to be cautious but not so guarded that no woman would ever get past the fortress you want to keep around your heart."

"If you say so. Thanks for talking to me, Lucky Charm, I mean Dr. Wyndham." He looked at his watch. "I still have fifteen minutes left on the clock I could use to talk to you, but I have to get ready to head to the venue, so I have to let you go now. Count the unused minutes as a tip from me. Thanks for your services. Enjoy the rest of your night."

"You, too." She let her words trail off hearing the dial tone.

***

The married men at the table eyes trailed the route their wives took to go to the bathroom.

"Fellas, it's just a bathroom break for them. They'll be back and you're going home with your wives tonight. No need to stare them down like the vultures you are." Darius laughed at himself.

Marcus turned around first to face Darius. "And that's why I'm watching her She's all mine and I love to take in every sight of her I can."

Darius looked at his watch as if it could tell him the date. "If I didn't know any better I'd swear it was Valentine's Day and y'all out here trying to score some brownie points with all of the caking you've been doing with your wives."

"I remember you all up in…" Vance let his words trail off as he stared at Darius' expectant face. He was about to recall all of the times he caught Darius flirting with and ogling Kim, but he thought better than bring her up. He knew Kim was a sore spot for Darius.

"What? What were you gonna say?" Darius asked with a half-smile on his face waiting to respond to Vance with a joke.

"Nothing, man." Vance cleared his throat and changed the subject. "Man, you killed your set tonight. Y'all have to be doing good if this is the second time you all have circled back around to Chicago."

Not wanting to run away from Vance's unsaid thought, a beat passed before Darius surmised what

Vance might have said to him. "Yeah, you changed the subject, but I think I know what you were going to say earlier."

"Nothing, man."

"Nah, it's cool. Say what you were gonna say. I know it was about Kim. I got on y'all for caking with your wives and of course, your comeback was gonna be to put me on blast for how I used to be with Kim. It's cool. She was worth all of the attention I gave her plus so much more."

All of the gentleman at the table waited to see what Darius would do next. In the past, the mere mention of Kim either caused him to blow up or leave. For him to bring her up, they honestly didn't know what to expect, what reaction they'd get from him.

"So you're cool with talking about her?" Anthony asked, with a raised brow.

"Yeah man, I am. I've been seeing a grief counselor and she's been helping me through it."

"What?" Vance stopped his glass from touching his lips and put it back down on the table. "You have? That's good, D." Vance extended his hand and gave Darius a fist bump.

"Yeah, Dr. Wyndham is good at what she does."

"How long have you been seeing her?" Andrew asked.

"Well, I haven't actually seen her face to face since our first visit, but it's been a few months. We either talk on the phone or video conference our sessions."

"Why didn't you tell us?" Marcus asked.

"Because it ain't none of your business." Darius laughed and took a quick swig of his bourbon.

"Man, whatever. I know between Marcus, Anthony, and myself, one of us call or text you at least once a week to check up on you, and you've never said you were seeing her. When we ask how you are, you just give us a basic 'okay' and after catching up on our lives, you rush off the phone," Vance said.

"Because, like I said, it's none of y'all business." Darius laughed again. "For real though, it took me a while to admit I needed to see someone, and when I did, I randomly picked her name from a web search. When I first went to see her, I was reluctant to talk to her, but she's so good at what she does that she helped me to open up and has been helping me really deal with losing Kim. She saved me from getting fired from the tour."

"Wow, she whipped you in shape like that?" Anthony asked. "You were hella funny tonight, back to the old Darius. And as ugly as you are, smiling again looks good on you. You've done it a few times since we've been sitting here."

The table sat quiet, waiting to hear Darius's comeback to Anthony. He soon took a quick sip of his drink and then looked at Anthony. "You know I could roast you, right?" He tilted his head in Anthony's direction. "But you've lived a rough enough life having to look at that mug of yours in the mirror every day."

Andrew, Vance, and Marcus let out hearty laughs before finally composing themselves and tuning back in to hear Anthony's retort, if any.

"Man, you know I ain't never been ugly a day in my life," Anthony said.

"Neither have I," Darius quipped.

The fellas' residual laughter subsided when Vance said, "Good to see you back or at least getting back to your old self. We were worried about you for a while."

"Me too." Darius chuckled to himself. "But like I said, Dr. Wyndham is a lifesaver. She's almost become my lifeline. I talk to her pretty much before every show. Except for tonight." He sat back in his seat with his glass in his hands and his shoulders slumped. He emptied the last of the contents in his mouth then placed it back down on the table.

"What just happened?" Vance asked.

"What?" Darius asked, questioning the fellas stares at him.

"You were joking and straight talking about how this doctor you've been seeing has been helping you, but your smile faded and mood changed after you said you hadn't talked to her today," Marcus said.

Vance raised a high eyebrow at Darius.

"It's nothing really. It's just that over the past week, I've done four shows including tonight's. Like I said, I was talking to her before almost all of my shows, but this past week, she hasn't answered any of my calls."

Vance leaned forward in his seat and eyed Darius a while before he said, "My brother, you've got it bad for her, don't you?"

"What?" Darius sat up straight in his seat. "No, it's nothing like that. I told you she's good at what she does. The strategies she gives me to deal with it all, her calming professionalism put me back on track with my comedy. I've gotten used to talking to her before the shows. She's like my lucky charm. So it's just been noticeable this past week not to chat with her."

Andrew cleared his throat. "I know I'm still new to the fold, but if I may butt in, I'd just like to agree with Vance," he looked around at the other guys around the table, "and judging from the nods and knowing looks from the other guys, yeah, you got it bad, my dude."

"Thanks, Andrew, for the confirmation," Vance said. "Maybe he'll believe you before us. You said earlier that y'all video chat as well, right?"

"Yeah," Darius said.

"So this therapist is talking to you what, at least three times a week, video chatting you and all and you're trying to sit there with a straight face and tell us that you don't want her? That there's nothing going on between you two?" Anthony asked.

"With a straight face I'm telling you that's exactly the case. She's kind of become like a good friend to me over these past months."

"Yup, like I thought. If you're looking at her like a friend, so you say, I can easily see her wanting more from you. You know it pisses women off when you friend zone them and they want to be more."

"What? She's been nothing but professional with me. I don't get that she wants me from any of her actions or words."

"And because you're clueless about your interest in her stands to reason why your clueless that she likes you," Vance said.

"Who likes who?" Pam asked in a stark tone as she took her seat next to her husband.

Darius cleared his throat and snubbed his nose, hoping the gentleman understood his silent plea to end their conversation.

Vance clearly understood him as he held his hand up. "Waiter, we're ready to order."

19

Pam

Pam shook her head. *I should've told him the moment I found out. The fact that Monica and Renee knows and he doesn't is just wrong, plain wrong. I've let this omission of a lie go on for far too long.*

"Pam, Pam?"

"Hunh?" Her mother's voice jarred her thoughts.

"I said will you pass me the macaroni already. You alright, sweetie? I've been asking for it for forever," Eilene said.

"Sorry, Momma." Pam passed her mother the porcelain bowl filled with macaroni and cheese.

"You okay?" Sitting next to her, Vance leaned in and whispered in her ear.

She looked at him with a weak smile. "Yeah, I'm okay."

"You sure?" His bushy yet naturally trimmed brow raised.

"Yes." She leaned forward and pecked him on his lips.

"I love it," Eilene exclaimed. "All of my babies *here* with their spouses."

Pam's father cut his eyes at his wife. "Eilene, don't start. They're grown. They have the right to do and go wherever they want to in life."

She stared directly at him before fixing her stare on Pam and Vance. "I know y'all are grown, but you just can't move away."

Pam and her mother's relationship had come a long way and made it possible for her to confess to her about Vance's job offer in Memphis. Of course, her mother was against it and that only made Pam feel bad knowing that Vance still wanted to take the position. Knowing her mother quite well, she let out a deep, long sigh and braced herself for the dramatics she was sure her mother was about to display.

With pleading eyes for a rescue, she looked over at her brothers who merely smirked and shrugged their shoulders knowing no one could stop Eilene Robinson when she got started.

Eilene finished chewing her food, wiped her mouth with a napkin she snatched from the table, and fixed her stare on Pam and Vance again. "You two are trying to leave me and all of this love." She waved her hands as if they were wands over the table. "Your brothers live here with their beautiful wives and children, but you wanna go start your lives somewhere else."

"Momma, it's not even like that," Pam mumbled.

"I mean you two rushed off and eloped and didn't even give me the chance to plan your wedding, witness my only daughter walk down the aisle in my old wedding dress that I just know you would've looked so stunning in."

Pam and her father stared at each other in confusion.

Eilene cocked her head at Pam. "So you wouldn't have worn my dress? You think it's ugly or something?"

"Momma, no. I didn't say that."

"Oh, okay. But like I was saying—"

"No, not like you were saying. Will you cut the dramatics already?" Mr. Robinson said. "Pam and Vance are grown and can make their own decisions. Let them decide what's best for them. Let's just support whatever it is they decide," He said, staring at his wife.

"But, Tony. You're comfortable with your only daughter moving so far away. Having kids of her own that we won't get to see on the regular. Will they even know us?" Eilene looked at Pam. "And what about the sisterhood? You all are as strong as gorilla glue. You would leave them, too?"

"Momma, I already told you we're not moving." Pam shifted her eyes to her father who sat across the table from her. She hoped the silent plea would cause her father to direct the conversation elsewhere, but the apologetic way he looked at Vance made her turn her attention to him.

The sad look in his eyes ate at her. She felt sick.

"Excuse me, guys." She gripped her stomach as she jumped up from the table and rushed to the bathroom on the second floor.

"I'll go check on her," Vance said and left the table. He saw what direction she headed and his long, muscular legs mounted the steps two at a time until he reached the top in mere seconds.

He heard Pam throwing up just beyond the cracked door down the hall and ran to it, pushing it wide open. He found his wife crouched in front of the toilet with her dark brown natural curls covering her face to her chin. Her body jerked forward as she apparently heaved up everything that was in her into the toilet.

"Pam, baby." He knelt down beside her and rubbed her back as he pushed her hair out of the way. "What's wrong? Was it the food again? Do we need to get you to a doctor? Are you allergic to something?"

She spit one last time into the toilet before she tried to stand up.

Vance practically lifted her off the floor by her waist before he settled her back on her feet. "Come here." He tried to pull her in for a hug, but she pushed him back some.

"Vance, I need to rinse my mouth out."

"Sorry."

She leaned down over the sink and went through cycles of filling her mouth with water and spitting it out before she was satisfied the taste of bile was no longer there. She splashed water on her face and when she reached for a hand towel she knew was rolled up on a rack nearby, Vance's hand was already outstretched with the towel in it.

"Thanks," she said, the towel muffling her voice. She looked up at him. "I'm sorry."

"You're sorry? For what? You're the one sick that's been sick off and on for a while. We need to get you to a doctor. Come on." He turned and pulled her arm to guide her out of the bathroom, but she stopped him with her voice.

"No, Vance, I don't need to go to a doctor. I already know what they'll say." She bit the inside of her jaw.

The tables had turned. She had been holding on to something, a big something, she knew she should've told him a long time ago.

He turned back to her and cocked his head. "What will they say? I hate to say this, but please don't tell me that you've been pulling a Kim on me. You're sick and didn't wanna tell me because you didn't want me to worry." He faced her fully, drew her in closer to him, and cupped her face with his big hands.

Looking from afar, one might not be able to tell if his hands were even on her face. They were both the same milk chocolate complexion.

"No, it's nothing like that." She looked up at him with unshed tears glossing her eyes.

"Well, what is it then?" The pitch in his voice elevated.

In all of her years of waiting for this particular moment, she never imagined doing it after a puke fest in a bathroom in her parents' house.

"Vance, I'm pregnant." She tried to look away from him as a tear fell but he kept a firm yet gentle hold on her face, forcing her to look up at him.

His eyes widened and his mouth stood ajar for what seemed like an eternity to Pam before he finally spoke. "You're pregnant?"

"Yes." More tears fell.

"So why are you crying about it? You don't want the baby?"

The questioning alarm in his deep, normally smooth voice made her brace one arm around his waist and the other on his elbow. "That's not it, Vance, not at all. I want this baby more than anything.

I fell in love with it the day I found out I was pregnant." She smiled wide.

"Wait, when was that?"

She bit her bottom lip and averted eye contact with him.

"Pam, how far along are you? How long have you known that you're pregnant? And why haven't you told me before now?" The inner corners of his brows met at the middle of his forehead as he looked down at her and took a step back.

She bit her bottom lip as she looked up at him. "Well, remember that day I made you fess up about the job offer for Memphis?"

"Pam." His nostrils flared and his eyes widened. "You knew then? That was almost two months ago. You've known you've been pregnant all of this time and didn't bother to tell me?" He took another step back from her but she closed in on him until his back was pressed against the bathroom door.

She circled her arms around his waist and looked up at him trying to will him to look at her.

He finally did. "I can't believe you've been pregnant all this time and didn't tell me. Why'd you keep this from me?"

"I'm sorry. When I first suspected it, I took a home pregnancy test and it came out positive."

"I should've known then."

"I know. I just wanted to make sure I really was before I got either of our hopes up high."

"But I should've been at the doctor with you when you did find out." His mouth was tight as he stared away from her.

"Vance, baby," she said, touching his chin and directing his face towards hers. "Vance, I'm sorry. I see just how easy or difficult, depending on the way you looked at it, it was for you to stall on telling me about the job offer. You wanted to do it when you thought the time was right and so did I when telling you about this." She looked down and rubbed her belly. "I just wanted to know for sure before I told you. I was gonna tell you that day I questioned you about the Memphis offer, but it just didn't seem like the right time. I wanted to tell you at an upbeat, happy time, not the way it's been lately."

"Baby, the right time was when you found out. I can't believe you've kept this from me for so long." He stared at her with a harshness she had never seen before.

Tears stained her face again.

"I know, but then Renee came back sad with news of not meeting her son and Monica bearing it all about Keith not being there for her, I just decided to put my announcement on the backburner."

He looked at her with a fierce intensity a beat longer before his features softened and he began to wipe away her tears with the pads of his thumbs. He leaned down and placed a soft, tender kiss on her lips.

When he pulled back from her, he could see her mouthing "thank you" to him.

"Baby, those are your friends, your sisters, but this is about us."

"I know, but they're a part of me, too. I saw the way you looked when my mother said with certainty that we weren't going to move, but now I hope you understand why I just can't do it. I'd be leaving the sisterhood, my family, and the baby, our baby, would not get the chance to be around the people we love the most.

"Not only would the baby not be around my friends and family, but don't you think Marcus would want our child to grow up with his kids, and what about your mom? You know she's been waiting for you to have kids for forever. I always dreamed of the sisterhood raising all of our kids together like brother and sisters. That can't happen with us in Memphis. I want you to be happy, too, but leaving everyone here and me raising the baby alone in Memphis, that makes me sad." She looked in his onyx hued eyes hoping to see his understanding. A headache surfaced in her and she decided to look away from him and place her head on his chest.

With the firm grip she had on him, he had no choice but to wrap his arms around her and rub her back to try and comfort her.

He leaned down to kiss her forehead and then said, "I understand your view. You know I really want the position in Memphis, but making sure the love of my life is happy is more important to me." He sighed. "If this opportunity came along, I'm certain, hoping, another one like it or better will come along again."

She heard what he said but the lack of enthusiasm in his voice let her know he may not have believed what he said after all. The sentiment, his valiant gesture didn't seem to reach his heart.

20

Monica

"Okay, God, I'mma try to make things right with my wife tonight. Please give me the words to say and the ear to hear when she speaks. Help us to reconnect and love one another like never before," Keith said to himself as he placed the two plates filled with food he'd made on the table in the kitchen.

He was grateful that his mom had agreed to watch the twins. Monica took them over to his parents' house and it gave him an excuse and the opportunity to prepare the house and set the mood as he had.

The alarm chimed and he knew the front door had opened. His eyes traveled the dark hallway save the votive candles lining it. He had balanced placing the perfect blend of candles and roses that created the pathway that would hopefully lead Monica right to him.

She was into the frou-frou girly stuff, so hopefully his setup would warm her heart and ease her into listening to him.

"Keith?" Monica asked, waddling down the hallway towards the kitchen, towards him.

He smiled as he met her at the meeting ground where the hallway ended and the kitchen area began.

"What is all of this?" She eyed him warily before looking past him at the table he had set with the plates filled with pasta, breaded chicken breasts, broccoli, and a jar of pickles where she presumed was her seat. She looked back at him.

"This is for you. This is for us." He gripped her hands, pulling them into his and then up to his lips. His full lips grazed her knuckles as he stared into her eyes. "This is hopefully the beginning of making up with you. Asking you to forgive me for shutting you out, for neglecting you and the kids, grieving in the selfish way I did."

Her eyes glossed over.

He caressed her cheek with one hand and her eyes closed and fluttered as tears streamed her face.

He swiped at her tears.

"I'm sorry, baby, for being a jerk." He leaned in and kissed her nose, then placed a soft kiss to her lips.

He wrapped his arms as best as he could around her lower back given how wide her almost nine months pregnant frame was. He rubbed her back trying to sooth her as her shoulders shook and soft sobs escaped her lips.

"I'm sorry. I was wrong that it took me so long to get to this point. But these past few weeks of you not bothering to question me about coming to bed, helping out with the kids, or saying anything to me, I knew I needed to get my act together before I lost you, too. Losing Kim and trying to get past it is the hardest thing I've ever had to do in my life, but, baby, when it really hit me that I might lose you, too, I knew I had to make things right."

Her sobs grew louder and he pulled her closer to him. "I didn't go to an actual therapist or counselor, but I did talk to Marcus, Pam's brother-in-law, a few times and he's prayed with me and has been a listening ear."

She pushed him off her and wiped away her tears. "I was supposed to be your listening ear."

"I know, and I'm sorry for not trusting you in that way, baby."

"I've needed you all of this time. You didn't just lose a sister, I lost one of my best friends." She huffed. "I bet these twins," she rubbed her belly, "will look just like you, as much as I've cried over you. Do you know how tired I am of crying?"

"I'm sorry. I can only imagine how tired you are. I'm sorry for it all. I am. And I'm hoping they'll look just like their beautiful mother and not their stupid father. Can you forgive me?" The sincerity in his eyes and the downward curve of his full lips pleaded with her.

"Ugh." She punched him in his arm. "Of course I forgive you, but no matter what happens in our lives again, you better not ever push me away and shut me out like this again." She punched him again.

He smiled. "I won't. Come here, girl." He clasped her face with both of his hands and pulled her in for a kiss that lit every ember of the fire he had burning inside for her. Clearly, she felt the same because the way she moaned as his expert tongue explored her mouth said she was just as in tune with him as he was with her.

When catching their breaths became a necessity, he finally pulled back from her, but not before placing sensual kisses all over her face. "Mo?" he said against her lips and gripping her backside. "Can we take this to the bedroom or the couch at least?"

He deepened their kiss and her arms secured around his neck as he began walking her backwards down the hallway.

With heavy lidded eyes, she pulled at the collar of his shirt and tried to guide him onto her, but he stopped, hovering over her.

"You know the last time you were this far along, you had to be on top."

"Yeah, you're right."

He tried to stand but her grip on his collar tightened as she screamed aloud, "Keith."

"I know, baby, it's been a long time for us, but I promise to do you right. Just loosen up your grip on my shirt and we'll get this right." He went to lift up again but was jerked down once more by the collar of his shirt.

"Keith," Monica blurted out as if she were trying to speak over a live band at a packed concert. "Keith, my water just broke and the contractions are killing me."

"What? You're in labor?" His eyes widened as if he were a first-time dad, nervous and unsure of what to do next.

"Yes, now get me up and get me to the hospital." She squeezed his shirt tighter and tried to breathe through another contraction.

He choked. "I. Can't. Breathe." His dark skin kept him from changing colors, but the wideness of his eyes and veins popping at his neck attested to his limited breathing capacity.

"Just get me up," she said finally letting him go.

He stood up and rubbed his throat as he gasped for air. He worked to get his breathing under control as he helped her up from the couch.

She took quick, short breaths as he supported her back and she wobbled from the couch to the front door. "My bag, there." She pointed to a gray diaper bag near the door before Keith had pushed her out of it.

"Okay." He kept his hand on her back and stretched to grab the bag. "Got it," he said before standing upright, grabbing his keys, and locking the door behind him.

The door closed and on the other side of it she screamed, and then he screamed as she almost broke his hand gripping it, trying to brace through another contraction.

21

Renee

"Talk to me." Andrew squeezed her hand and stared at her.

Renee slowly pulled her attention away from the clouds she was staring at to focus on his face. As if it were her first time seeing him, butterflies swarmed her stomach, while she stared into his intense, dark brown eyes. He was incredibly handsome to her. "I can't believe this is finally happening." She pulled her hand from his and covered her face, squeezing her arms tight against herself.

He leaned in close to her. "Renee," he pulled her hands from her face, "talk to me."

Sher turned to face him and with their closeness, she could feel his breath on her face.

"Are you gonna kiss me?" She stared into his eyes.

He smirked as he stared at her. "I want to, but I know you'd probably freak out if I did it in public."

She surprised him when she leaned in and pressed her lips against his. Their noses rubbed together as Renee tilted her head to gain better access to his mouth.

He opened his mouth and she deepened the kiss before she suddenly pulled back and covered her mouth in shock.

"What?" He laughed.

"I can't believe I just did that. In public."

"I know, right? You initiate a kiss and in public? What would the church mothers say?"

She covered her face and chuckled before she swatted at him. "You're silly. I'm so full of nervous energy. I can't believe that after years of wondering about him and then months of trying to meet him, out of the blue, my son, Isaiah, finally agrees to meet me."

"I'm happy for you." He kissed her cheek and leaned back some to watch the glow radiating from her. "Why the frown all of a sudden?" he asked, noticing the downward curve of her mouth.

"I don't know, I just thought about leaving so sudden after Monica went into labor. We all were there for the first set of twins' births. I wanted to be there for this set, too."

"I know you did, but when you got the call this morning from the Browns saying Isaiah burst in their room saying he was ready to meet you, you and I both know there was no way you were going to postpone meeting him to stay around until Monica gave birth."

"You're right." She smiled.

"Life is not linear. It's okay to experience your joy while someone else is experiencing theirs."

"I know, it's just that everything has changed since she left." Renee leaned onto his shoulder and he pulled her into his embrace and kissed her forehead.

He loved her with everything that was in him and would show her just how much in due time.

"I know that's still a lot for you, but I've seen you over these months. You are strong, Renee. And you'll continue to thrive. You all like to say that Kim was the toughest, but given the life you've lived, you're built Ford tough, too."

Tough. I ran when confronted by the one man I said would never make me flinch again. I'm not tough. Disgusted with her thoughts, she tried to pull away from Andrew, but he kept her close to him.

"Renee, what is it? There's something you're not telling me about." He allowed her to pull away from him as she sat up and looked at him.

She promised Kim and herself that she would be strong and not let anyone back her into a corner without fighting her way out of it. She thought she had done that when she stood face to face with Ted in the restaurant and told him that he'd never meet their son, have the chance to do him the way he'd done her. Her latest goal was to reconnect with her son by any means necessary and no matter how long it took, but looking back, maybe staying away from D.C. for the months she'd been away was the coward still rising up in her. She had a voice and she could at least use it now to tell Andrew the truth. She took a deep breath. "There's something I've been keeping from you, from everyone."

"What is it?" The frantic look on her face and the stall in her voice, enraged and unnerved him.

"The real reason why I came back to Chicago without meeting my son was because I ran into Ted the night before I came back."

"Ted?" His jaws tensed, his nostrils flared, and his already defined biceps flexed though his fitted shirt. His physique had him mirroring the incredible Hulk when he got mad.

"Calm down." She grabbed his knee, squeezing it, but then buried her face in her hands. She was nervous and scared of what Andrew might do.

Luckily for them, no one sat in the aisle chair to the left of him, so he had room to move, compose himself as needed. He leaned in close to her, pulling her hands away from her face and said, "Renee, you have nothing to be embarrassed about or anything like that. Why didn't you tell me before now?" He stared at her, his dark brown eyes imploring her to say something. When she didn't, he fell back into his seat and let out a sigh and rubbed his hand over his face. He took another deep breath, calming himself before he leaned over to her again.

"Renee, baby, I'm not mad at you, if that's what you're thinking. Stop shaking, don't cry." He pulled her into him, rubbed her arm, and pushed her hair out of her face. "I'm angry that you had to deal with him at all, in the past and recently. I wish you would've told me the minute it happened. I would've found him and handled him."

She sat up, tears streaming her face, and looked at him. "That's why I didn't tell you. Drew, I see how protective you are of me. I love it, I really do, but I didn't want you to do something that would get you into trouble."

He let out a deep sigh. "I know, but this dude can't keep going on thinking you have no one on your side. I'm certain Keith doesn't know, right? He and I talked about how we would handle Ted if he ever bothered you again."

Her head cocked slightly and her eyes widened as she stared at him. "See, this is why I didn't tell you all, yet."

He balled his fists. "Renee, obviously this punk, Ted, is crazy. You can't handle him alone. And wait, you ran into him, where?"

"Well, I didn't run into him. I think he was following me. Remember that day we were in the antique shop?"

"Yeah," he said, his thick, dark eyebrows furrowed.

"Well, I thought I saw him across the street when I was looking out the window. That's why I wanted to go back to the hotel and lay down all of a sudden. The thought of seeing him shook me."

He squeezed her hand and his handsome face tensed again.

"And then—"

"And? You saw him more than once and didn't say anything to me?"

"Drew, I wasn't sure if it was him. I just felt like someone was following me when I would venture out into D.C. And then the last night I met with Mrs. Brown, when I got up to leave the restaurant, he stopped me."

"I knew I shouldn't have left you there by yourself. Did he put his hands on you?"

Renee could hear his heavy breaths of anger. She avoided eye contact with him for a second because she didn't know what she'd see when she looked into them—rage, disappointment, pity. She took a deep breath and finally fixed her eyes on his. "Drew, he didn't touch me." She brought her hand up to his face and caressed it, trying to calm him down.

He closed his eyes briefly and took a deep breath. He was trying to keep his cool in front of her. Her sweet voice forced his eyes open.

"He didn't touch me, he just stopped me from moving, said he overheard everything I'd said to Kristen, and that if I was going to get the chance to meet our son, he wanted that chance, too."

Andrew pulled her into him. "I'm sorry you had to deal with him alone again, but trust me, that won't ever happen again."

She leaned into him for a while, taking in the scent of his cologne. She'd smelled it so often on her that when she asked him what brand and he told her, it sent her on an internet search to see exactly what ingredients was in it. It mixed with his natural scent to make him smell like only he could smell. The lemon, bergamot, and orange blossom combination of the cologne always left her secretly swooning over him and left her anticipating when she'd get close enough to him again just to take in his essence.

It was that crisp aroma of his that made her snuggle up closer to him at the moment and cling to the comfort he provided her rather than the dismay she had been feeling.

He interlaced his hands with hers and pulled her even closer to him trying to express his covering of her through his embrace. He leaned in some more and whispered against her forehead, "Renee, I'll always be here for you. Believe that, always."

***

Andrew got out of the Uber, rounded the car, and pulled Renee close to him. He surveilled their surroundings as if he were the CIA guarding the President of the U.S. He peered over his shoulder as he ushered her to the restaurant door. "Good thing you switched from the hotel you had been staying at. If the fool was following you before, he may still be lurking around it to see when he'll spot you again."

"Drew, you've held me to your side since we got off the plane, checked in to the hotel, and kept me close to you on the Uber ride over here."

"All of which I enjoyed." He winked. "But that's the way it will be whenever you're here. That fool needs to know you're not alone."

Knowing her, he leaned down and planted a quick yet consuming kiss to her lips, squashing the protest he was sure she was ready to make of him fussing over her.

Her eyes fluttered as she tore herself away from his lips. "Thanks."

"Always my pleasure." He smiled and locked hands with her as they crossed the restaurants threshold. He leaned down and whispered to her. "It's also a good thing the Browns agreed to meet you at this new restaurant rather than the one you used to meet up at."

"Drew," she said in a pleading voice as she eyed him.

He chuckled. "Renee, get used to this. You won't ever tell me that a man threatened you and I carry on as if everything is okay. I already felt protective of you before the incident, but now, woman, my hawk eyes are focused on you, and anyone who tries you will feel the wrath of my love for you."

She'd always prayed that if she ever allowed herself to love again that the man would love her the way Christ loved the church and gave himself for it. Andrew constantly exhibited that kind of love towards her. While the nagging thoughts of ever running into Ted again or him trying to gain access to their son loomed over her, knowing that she was finally meeting her son face to face that night moved her. The strength and love radiating from the man clasping her hand was more than what she had ever hoped for in a man. He had carved the smile on her face and the inexplicable joy in her heart. "I love you."

"I love you more." He looked down at her.

"Hello, table for two?" the waiter asked.

"No, the rest of our party should already be here."
She had talked with the Browns and they had agreed
that it would best if they brought Isaiah to the
restaurant first, and then Renee and Andrew arrive
after they were settled in.

Renee pointed to the table where she saw Mr.
Brown's head peeking above everyone else's at the
table. "That's our party over there." She took a deep
breath and Andrew squeezed her hand.

"You got this." He leaned in to her.

Although she had Andrew's loving assurance
around her, she still shuddered as she made her way
to the table. She'd prayed for the day she would meet
him. In some conjured scenarios of him meeting him,
she would look at him and he would run into her arms
admitting how much he missed her. In others, when
they met and she would try to hug him, he would push
away from her as she held onto him for dear life
asking for his forgiveness. But now, her tongue was
heavy and her breathing was labored as she stared at
him. He was the perfect blend of her, Kim, and Keith.

"Renee." Mrs. Brown stood and hugged her. She
could tell she was shaken. "It's okay. Your chance has
finally come."

Andrew helped Renee in her seat and shook
hands with Mr. and Mrs. Brown before he nodded and
shook Isaiah's hand.

Renee was still stunned, unable to speak.

"Hi," Isaiah finally said, staring at Renee.

"Hi." Her word came out shaky and her tears flowed freely.

"How are you?" Isaiah asked.

Renee chuckled and shook her head as she wiped her face. "Oh my goodness. I'm so sorry. I'm trying not to cry, but you're here. I'm here. We're here together, almost fourteen years later. You're talking to me. You're so handsome and so mature. I should've been the one to speak to you first."

He shrugged his shoulders before looking to his mother and father. He looked back at Renee, "It's cool."

She laughed and cried at the same time. "I'm so sorry, you guys. I just can't believe that this moment is finally here." She wiped her face one last time and shook her head as if trying to control her haywire emotions with the action. With wide eyes, she looked to Kristen for assurance and when she smiled and nodded at her, Renee knew it was okay for her to continue.

"Isaiah, is it okay to call you Isaiah, or do you like to be called something else?"

"My friends call me Izzy, but you can call me whatever."

Renee would call him whatever he wanted her to call him. She was just glad and ever grateful that he was talking to her *and* making eye contact with her.

She'd been around enough kids, especially boys his almost fourteen years of age to know how withdrawn and dismissive they could be when confronted by their estranged parents. His willingness to talk to her gave her so much hope and yet she was still filled with worry wondering just how and if he would receive all that she had to say to him.

"Okay, Izzy." She smiled. "Let me know if anything I say upsets you and I'll slow down or change the subject until you're ready to talk about it again, but I want to be honest with you about it all. Cool?"

"Sure." He shrugged his shoulders.

She took another deep breath prepping to share the short yet detailed version of why she gave him up for adoption to begin with. "Izzy, I was just a naïve college student when I met your father…"

Twenty minutes later and a few head nods from Isaiah, Renee was done with her retelling of why she had to give him up for adoption.

"As I've said before, because it's so true, I was never really me over the years because of my guilt of giving you up, but I felt like it was the only choice to save you from him. Do you understand why I had to?"

Everyone was silent at the table awaiting Isaiah's response. He sat hunched over, jabbing a French fry into a pile of ketchup on his plate. "Yeah, I get it," he finally said, and then looked up at Renee.

With her hand flat on her chest, she let out a loud sigh of relief as she stared at him. Water brimmed her eyelids again before her face shimmered with tears.

"You just don't know how much I've hoped and prayed that if and when we came face to face and you let me share my story with you, that you'd forgive me." She reached across the table and patted his hand, when he didn't flinch, she muffled her cry with her other hand. She stifled her cry just enough to speak. "You are such a strong boy. You had every right to tell me you never wanted to see me. You could've kept telling your parents that you didn't want to meet me or talk to me, but you decided to anyway and I'm so grateful for it."

"Ms. Renee, you don't have to cry anymore. I was nervous about meeting you. Even though I knew my parents loved me I still wondered sometimes why my blood parents gave me away. One day last week, a YouTube video I was watching ended and one began where kids and parents were talking about what it was like for them growing up with their bad parents who adopted them. The video also showed parents who wished they'd done things differently to keep their kids and not give them up."

Renee smiled through her tears listening to how smart and well-spoken her Isaiah, her Izzy was.

"Before that video, I really didn't want to meet you, because I'm fine with my life and my parents, but I thought about how bad some of those kids had it with the people they were living with and the way some of the parents were trying to get them back but couldn't. It all made me think that maybe you were one of the good ones trying to connect with your kid." He bore an innocent look on his face. "It made me want to give you a chance. I wanna get to know you."

She sobbed at his admission but quickly composed herself and looked at him. "Can I hug you?"

"Sure." He shrugged his shoulders and stood up.

Andrew stood and helped the shaky Renee out of her seat. She peered down at her son as he leaned into her. His head rested on her chest as his hands braced around her waist. Her arms dropped around him and she hugged him with all she had in her. It didn't matter to her who heard her sobs mixed with laughter as she squeezed him trying to channel all of the love she had inside of her into her hug.

"Ms. Renee, I can't breathe," Isaiah said, his voice muffled against her checkered shirt.

"I'm sorry." She chuckled and planted a quick kiss to his forehead before she finally released him from her embrace. She wiped her face and said, "I'm sorry, I'm a hugger and a kisser."

He chuckled. "That's okay, my mom is, too."

Although it stung a little, she wouldn't dare concern herself about the fact that he called her Ms.

Renee and Kristen his mom. The truth was, Kristen was the only mom he'd ever known. Renee was just the woman who had given birth to him, but he was willing to getting to know. Something of which she would be eternally grateful for.

They rejoined their seats and the table's energy shifted to cheer as Isaiah answered the questions Renee fired at him trying to get to know him more.

Renee had enough joy radiating around her to light the restaurant and the surrounding businesses if the electricity were to go out. That's just how much she was glowing, sitting across from her son as he talked about his friends, school, and all of the sports he played.

***

It was that joy, that celestial aura lighting up her face that had Ted's feet planted across the street staring at her for the past twenty minutes. It was that same innocence, peace that had drawn him to her at first.

He'd oddly took joy in getting a rise out of Renee the last time he saw her. But seeing her now, glowing the way she was, it burned him up to know that his actions led to the chain of events that ultimately forced Renee to give their son up for adoption.

He'd known Renee wouldn't fight him back the way some of his other girlfriends had in the past and he took full advantage of that when he was with her, pretty much controlling every aspect of her life, down to how she dressed, what she ate, and even who she could be around.

He saw a fighter in her that day he approached her in the restaurant and although he was smug with her and admittedly a bully when encountering her again, the time after that did him in. He looked for her again for a few weeks, going to all of the places he had seen her at since she'd been back in D.C., but when he got the nerve to go to the front desk of her hotel and ask for them to page her, the concierge telling him that she was no longer there shook him back to reality.

He'd sent her running again. That was not who he was supposed to be after his stint in prison. He had worked hard to rehabilitate himself, denounce the past that had made him the man he was. But life in the real world was much different than it had been ten years ago. He struggled keeping a job and was constantly at odds with his mother, whom he lived with.

The weight of his new reality played into why he antagonized her. His world wasn't right, yet she looked so peaceful and adjusted in hers. But that was no excuse for his behavior. He'd promised himself that the first chance he ever got with her, he'd make things right with her, but like the fool of his past, he bullied her.

But tonight, seeing her brought him the chance to make things right with her once and for all. He wouldn't rush her in the restaurant again, he'd wait until she was heading out before he approached her.

***

"Well, I'm so happy that you two finally had the chance to connect," Kristen said.

"I am, too." Renee bubbled over with joy.

"Not sure when you go back to Chicago, but if you want to, you and Andrew can come to his game on Saturday and maybe we can go out for pizza or something afterwards. I'm sure it'll be a celebration of his victory. This champ here always wins." Josh rubbed Isaiah's head.

"Definitely. What colors should I wear?"

Isaiah face palmed himself. "Oh no, you're like her, too. The embarrassing Mom in the stands."

Everyone laughed except for Isaiah as he continued to shake his head.

"I'll try not to be," Renee said, her smile almost cracking her face. She embraced Kristen and Josh one last time before they headed to the door.

Isaiah was close behind them before he turned around and rushed back over to Renee to give her a quick hug. He pulled back from her and looked into eyes that looked much like his. "See you Saturday, Ms. Renee." He looked to Andrew. "You, too?"

"You bet." Andrew extended his hand for a fist bump to which Isaiah returned before he rushed off to catch up with his parents.

"Bye, Izzy," Renee said to his fleeting back.

When she saw them walk past the window outside of the restaurant, she turned and faced Andrew with the biggest expression of shock on her face. "Pinch me."

"What?" His eyebrows drew closer together as he frowned.

"Pinch me. I need to see if this moment is real, if I really just sat and had dinner with my son. He hugged me, he talked to me, he smiled at me." She squealed but then covered her mouth observing the attention she was drawing to herself.

He leaned down and pecked her lips. "I won't pinch you, but yes, all you said just happened. Let's get you out of here and you can jump around the suite as much as you'd like and not have to worry about the stares of others." He looked over his shoulder at a couple he knew had been snooping on their conversation the entire time they were there.

"Okay, let's go." She grabbed her purse hanging on the chair and walked out hand in hand with

Andrew into the beautiful late summer evening in D.C.

Andrew only hoped that the surprise he had waiting for her back at the hotel could match at least half of the joy he saw all over her after meeting her son.

He pulled her hand up to his lips and kissed it before they set into their stride after they exited the restaurant.

She stopped.

"Renee, come on," he said, pulling her hand. He was still walking and moved over just enough to let the man heading in their direction get past them on the sidewalk.

The tall, rugged looking man stopped short of them and stared past Andrew.

Andrew snapped his neck back to see that Renee hadn't moved when he tugged on her hand again and she looked as if she had been frozen in place. The color had drained from her face and that glow he just saw her basking in was gone. "Renee?"

She said nothing but he saw where her eyes were trained and it made him look back at the man near them.

The man held his hands up. "Renee—"

Frustrated with his presence, him saying her name, she snatched her hand away from Andrew and screamed, "Leave me alone. Just leave me alone."

Andrew drew closer to her. "Renee, talk to me, baby." When she wouldn't speak, Andrew looked back at the man, without fully knowing, but putting everything together. Him knowing Renee's name and her reaction to him, he was convinced that the man that had approached them was Ted.

"I'll kill you." Andrew charged at him and pounced on the man without any concern for the quality of his life when he was done with him. "Don't you ever say her name again," Andrew said, punching Ted and threw him to the ground, choking him.

"Get off of me, man." Ted tussled under Andrew.

"Andrew. Drew," Renee screamed frantically. "Drew."

Andrew could only see the red bulls-eye that Ted had clearly painted on himself when he decided to approach Renee again. They were of the same height and build, but Andrew's rage fueled his strength and trumped that of Ted's as he straddled him and squeezed his throat tighter.

"Drew." Renee's piercing scream tried to penetrate the force field Andrew was cocooned in while he attacked Ted. "Drew."

Andrew's hold around Ted's neck tightened as Ted clawed at Andrew's hands trying to loosen their grip on him. He couldn't breath and was losing consciousness.

Ted's eyes bulged from his sockets as much as the veins visibly pulsed in Andrew's neck and arms.

"Drew, let him go."

The sweet plea from her was enough to finally bring him out of his haze of rage.

He looked down at Ted. "Don't you move."

Andrew jumped up but still towered over Ted as he rolled on his side coughing, flailing, and kicking for air.

Andrew stepped away from him, never taking his eyes off him. "Come on, Renee, let's go." He reached out until he connected his hand with hers and walked backwards, ushering her away from Ted. Never taking his eyes off him.

Ted wanted to use the moment wisely so he stood, rubbed his throat and worked to regain full use of his lungs. He called out to them. "Wait, I need to tell you something, Renee."

Hearing Ted say her name again and knowing how it shook her the first time, Andrew charged at him, ready to finish what he'd started, but Renee had a firm grip on his arm.

"Drew."

He knew if he tried to pull away from her, he'd probably hurt her in the process. That made him stay still.

With his hands up in surrender, Ted walked up to an arms-length of them. "Look, whoever you are," he looked to Andrew, "this is between me and Renee."

"No, you have nothing more to say to her." Andrew gritted his teeth and his nostrils flared.

Keeping her firm grip on Andrew's arm, Renee stepped beside him. "Drew, let's just ignore him and go."

Once again, the sweet plea in her voice calmed the rage in him. "Look, man, Ted, just stay the hell away from her, or I swear, I'll catch you when she's not around and there won't be anyone to stop what I do to you."

They walked away.

"I'm sorry." Ted yelled after them.

The sincerity in his voice halted Renee's feet.

"What are you doing, baby? Let's just go. You don't have to listen to another word from that clown."

"I know, Drew, but maybe I can make this the last time we ever have to speak." She looked at him and caressed his face, massaging the bulge in his tense jaws.

Andrew let out a gruff sigh and turned to face Ted. "You have three minutes to say whatever it is you have to say and then get away from my woman and stay away from her."

Ted kept his hands raised as a sign of good faith. He stepped forward.

"Stay back," Andrew ordered.

"I don't wanna have to yell to be heard so far away from y'all. I wasn't gonna harm or touch her when I first approached her and I won't now." He locked his hands behind his back and took slow steps toward them.

"That's close enough," Andrew said through clenched teeth.

"I see you have a fighter there, Renee." He smirked and nodded his head towards Andrew.

Andrew lurched towards Ted, but Renee kept him in place with her firm grip on his arm.

"I mean no harm, man, just saying I see she has someone by her side." He looked from Andrew to Renee. "Look, Renee, I'm sorry for the way I was towards you in the past. My first couple of years in prison, I was upset and blaming you for putting me there, but then with the help of others, I started looking in the mirror to see that I was the real problem. I thought I had the finger pointing out of my system, but I guess seeing you that day at the antique store triggered something in me I didn't know was still there.

"I grew up seeing my father and uncles be abusive to the women in their lives, and I thought that was the way I was supposed to be. That thinking made me treat you the way I did. I thought I had changed that thinking in prison. I told myself that if I ever saw you again, I'd make things right between us, apologize, but old habits die hard. I didn't treat you the way I should have when I approached you in that restaurant."

Andrew continued to flex his muscles, ready to pounce on Ted again if need be.

"I live not too far from here. I was walking by when I looked over and saw you in the restaurant with who I assumed to be our son?" He tilted his head at Renee.

She didn't answer his question.

"I get it. You should want to protect him. Standing outside of the restaurant seeing that genuine smile on your face talking to him, reminded me of the innocence I know I stole from you long ago."

Andrew squeezed Renee's hand trying to calm her trembling.

"I just wanted to say that I hope you can find it in your heart to forgive me for all of the wrong I've done to you. I promise I won't bother you again. And thank you for birthing that beautiful boy I saw tonight. I can only hope I'm able to connect with him one day the way you have. Good bye, Renee." Ted turned and walked away, but Renee's words stopped his tracks.

"I forgive you," Renee said to his retreating back.

Head low, he shook it hearing the sincerity in her voice. Even though he hoped for it, he kept walking not comprehending that after all he'd put her through she could still have joy and forgive him. It cemented the fact that she was a remarkable woman and he would be hard-pressed to ever find another like her.

Andrew watched Ted's path until he was no longer in sight. He turned to Renee and pulled her in his arms. He buried his chin in her soft, relaxed hair. "You okay?"

She squeezed him. "Yes."

The warmth in her voice made him pull back and with raised eyebrows looked in her eyes. "You sure?"

She smiled. "Yes."

"I don't understand how."

"I had to forgive him for what he did to me a long while ago. It was just his presence, him bringing up wanting to see our son that sent me haywire. I wasn't sure of his current actions, but I had to forgive his past actions to be able to live, to trust, to love you." She looked up at him with such tenderness in her eyes. "Besides, after reconnecting with Isaiah and you being here with me through it all, there's not much else that matters to me." She gave him a half smile as her mind flashed to how her joy could only be topped by Kim still being alive.

"You really are one amazing woman." He leaned down to kiss her and when their lips touched, he engaged her in a fiery experience. Their tongues tangled with such passion that Renee was forced to pull away from him on shaky legs.

"Whoa, you okay?" He laughed.

"Yeah," she said, squeezing her eyes tight trying to get rid of the twinkling stars she saw when they were kissing. When she had her bearings and her breathing had returned to a glimmer of normalcy, she looked up at him and said, "It's just that your kisses are my kryptonite."

"I like that. I like that." He smirked and went in for another kiss, but her hand to his chest kept him at bay.

"Simmer down." She smiled.

He laughed. "Okay." He pulled her hand up to his lips and kissed it before he pulled out his phone to order another Uber.

He sensed she needed time to take in what had already happened to her that night. He'd just have to schedule his plans he had back at the hotel for another day.

22

Pam

Two men—one short and stout, the other tall, dark, and strikingly handsome—entered the main office.

Shelly, the clerk, noticed them the same time Pam did. She stood and rounded her desk, extending her hand to them. "Hello, Mr. Perkins and Mr. Wade," she said, offering them a bright smile.

"Hello," the men said simultaneously.

"Mr. Sutherland is waiting for you all in his office."

Staring at the rows and columns of staff mailboxes in front of her, Pam's ears perked up. She knew all of the suits down at the central and district offices. Neither of them jogged her memory. She could have given them the benefit of doubt that they were new hires except for their short hellos giving way to the southern drawl in their voices.

"Right this way." Shelly extended her hand in the direction of the door, allowing them to walk ahead of her.

They paused and let her step in front of them to which she opened Vance's massive office door and they stepped in before her. "Okay," Shelly said over her shoulder as she closed the office door. She moseyed back to her seat and resumed her clerical duties.

Pam shuffled her way over to Shelly and leaned down to whisper since she didn't want any other office staff to hear her inquiry. "Who was that?" she asked, covering her mouth.

"Memphis school district's top guys," Shelly responded, offering Pam a wary smile. Jensen Academy's staff was a close-knit family. Pam knew the look Shelly was giving her. Shelly was not only aware that Memphis wanted him heading their schools, but that Pam was the reason he'd turn down their offer.

"See you later, Shelly," Pam said, walking away from her desk.

Shelly looked up at her. "Okay, Mrs. Sutherland, see you at clock out time."

Pam took slow steps towards the back door leading out of the office. Although Vance had doted on her since he found out she was pregnant and the news of it kept a smile on his face, she knew him well enough to know that he was putting up a front about how he really felt about declining the job offer.

The stacks of papers she found lying around the house at times grounded her suspicions. He was still diligent in outlining proposals and plans to turn schools and districts around as he had Jensen. She knew he was no longer settled with just being the principal at their school.

With that knowledge, she'd been beating herself up for not letting him be the leader of their family and make decisions he felt was best for them. She was causing him to choose her fears over his happiness.

In his office, Vance focused on the men seated in front of him. "Gentleman, I hate that you all came all the way up here to Chicago in hopes of changing my mind, but as I've said many times before, I just can't accept the position."

Pam was just past the slightly ajar back door of his office when she heard his words, the heaviness in his voice.

"I have to put my family first," Vance said.

She knew it wasn't heartburn that instantly engulfed her insides, but his last statement had stung and hit her right in the chest. He was willing to compromise for her, but was she willing to do the same for him, for them?

Not wanting to barge in, but no longer able to stomach the position she had put him in, she rushed around to the front door of his office, knocking on it and opening it at the same time.

Vance looked up to see the pensive expression on her face. And when she opened and closed her mouth several times without saying anything, he knew something was wrong with her. He rushed from behind his desk to her. "Pam, baby, you okay?" He leaned in closer to her and rubbed her stomach. "Is the baby okay?" He cradled her face and peered down at her, looking deep into her eyes.

"Yes, I'm fine and the baby is, too. Once again, I was on my way out the back door of the office and your second door wasn't fully closed." She pointed to the back door to show him the sliver of the opening.

He looked to where she pointed and then looked back at her.

"I couldn't help but overhear you tell the gentleman you wouldn't accept the position because you had to put your family first."

Vance pulled his hands from her face and dropped them to his sides.

"I hear the disappointment in your voice and see the sadness in your eyes whenever you have to repeat the fact that you had to turn down the offer. You're sacrificing your dream for my comfort, but what am I doing? What am I sacrificing?"

"You don't have to. It's my job to make you happy above all else."

"No, it's our job to make each other happy. I know you love Jensen, but you want more. You want to make a greater impact on kids, worldwide, if you can."

Vance couldn't refute her admission. He remained quiet.

"Although I hadn't said anything to you yet, Pastor Riley's message last week about embracing newness pricked my heart. It made me think about you accepting the job and us moving to Memphis being a new season for us. That and this baby baking in the oven."

He smiled.

"My mother will always be dramatic, whether we're here or there." They both chuckled. "She'll eventually get over the move. And even though the sisterhood has already dealt with so much, deep down, I know our bond can withstand the miles, especially if we're still holding on after Kim's death."

She stepped around him and stood near his desk to face the Memphis suits who had been subjected to their conversation the whole time. "Sorry, gentleman, for barging in on your meeting. I'm Vance's, Mr. Sutherland's wife, Pam Sutherland."

She extended her hand out to shake theirs as they stood and greeted her.

Vance just stood back watching what she'd do next.

"I'm so glad you all came up to see him. Your presence gave me the needed push to see that him accepting this offer is the best thing for our family. Since I've already overstepped my boundaries and crossed the lines of professionalism when I barged in here, let me make it worthwhile by saying that my husband will be taking the position." She smiled at them and then turned to stare at Vance's wide eyes trained on her.

Still standing and with hopeful, inquisitive expressions, Mr. Perkins and Mr. Wade turned to face Vance.

He stepped closer to them all, pulling Pam to his side, and with a wide grin showcasing his perfect set of white teeth said, "Yes, I accept the offer."

Mr. Perkins, the short and stout one of the duo, firmly gripped Vance's hand up and down and said with much cheer in his voice, "We're so glad to finally have you onboard." He released Vance's hand.

Mr. Wade immediately extended his hand to shake Vance's hand. "Indeed."

"And don't think you'll just be following him down there. We may not have known you by face when you first came in, but when scouting him, our thorough research revealed he was married to a stellar teacher. We have a teaching spot waiting for you in one of our finest schools," Mr. Perkins said.

Vance looked down at Pam with such admiration in his eyes that he couldn't wait to get her home and thank her for her change of heart.

"I'm looking forward to the move." She smiled. "I know Vance is the best man for the job. You all don't know it, but I'm pregnant, so I won't be able to take that promised teaching position until after I've had a lengthy maternity leave. But rest assured that my love for teaching will have me in that classroom in due time. Well, gentleman, I'll leave out the same way I came in. I have to rush to pick my students up from art now." She looked to Vance and winked. "See you later."

"Take care, Mrs. Sutherland," Mr. Perkins said, rejoining his seat.

"See you soon." Mr. Wade smiled and then, walked over to Vance's wall of accolades.

"Pam, wait up." Vance caught her arm before she stepped out of his office. He lowered his voice. "You sure about all of this?"

"Yes, I'm more than certain this is the right thing for us. I want you to be happy just as much as you want me to be happy. I just have to figure out a way to break the news of us moving to the sisterhood and to my mother." She sighed as she left his office.

***

Pam sat at her parent's dining room table, staring at her plate full of food. She was hungry but knowing what news she had to share with her parents and guessing how her mom would respond, she was antsy and unable to focus on eating.

She'd remedy that soon though because her unborn child was demanding to be fed.

"You alright?" Vance leaned into her.

"Yeah, let's just get this over with."

"You sure?" He raised a brow at her.

"We have no choice at this point." She feigned a smile. "We leave next week."

"Church was good, wasn't it?" Eilene didn't even let anyone at the table answer her before she turned her attention to her oldest son's wife. "Now tell your father-in-law what you told me about that youngest daughter of yours on the phone the other day," she said, smiling at her daughter-in-law.

Pam spoke up the minute her sister-in-law finished and when everyone's laughter subsided. "Mom, Dad, everyone, Vance and I have something to tell you."

Eilene's slanted, brown eyes, just like Pam's, widened and she gripped her husband's hand as she stared at Pam and Vance. "Go on. What do you have to tell us?" Her voice was bubbling over with glee.

"We're pregnant."

"Ahhh." Eilene screamed and jumped out of her seat and rushed to Pam's seat. She leaned over the back of the walnut stained dining table chair, wrapped her arms around her daughter's neck, and kissed her face as if she were covered with cotton candy. "I just knew it'd happen soon. Oh, my baby is finally having a baby." She kissed on Pam again.

"Mom… Mom, thanks."

"Eilene, get off of that girl." Pam's father chuckled and beckoned for his wife to return to her seat.

"Oh hush, Tony. My baby is having a baby. I can celebrate her all I want." She cocked her head at her husband.

"Congrats, sis," one of Pam's brothers called out.

"Yay, Auntie Pam," Pam's youngest niece said and those at the table chuckled.

"Stand up, Pam, let me see you." Eilene pulled on Pam's arm.

"Mom." Pam whined but stood as Vance pulled her seat back and moved over to help her get up.

Eilene's smile stretched wide across her dark brown face as she stared at her only daughter. Her eyes began to brim with unshed tears.

"Mom, don't cry." Pam's face crinkled.

"I can't help it. You're so beautiful and I just love you so much." She pulled Pam into her embrace. "Oh gosh, you've just made me so happy." She pulled back from her but gripped Pam's hands in hers. "I didn't get to plan your wedding so the baby shower has to be big. It'll be the best one ever thrown in Chicago." She spread her hands wide as her voice pitched high with excitement. "Even though it'll be months and months away, I still need all of the time I can get to plan it."

Pam took a deep breath and shook her head. She knew her mother would begin to take things overboard with planning and whatnot before she even knew all of the details.

"So, how far along are you? A few weeks, a month at most?" Eilene smiled, staring at Pam's stomach.

"No, ma'am. More like four months."

Eilene's eyes widened, her jaw slacked, and she dropped Pam's hands. "You've been pregnant for four months and didn't even bother to tell me?" Eilene stumbled back a little, clutching her chest.

Pam reached out to her. "Mom, are you okay?"

"She's fine. Just perfecting her acting skills," Pam's father said loud before shaking his head.

"Pamela Shanice Sutherland, have you really been pregnant all of this time and didn't bother to tell me?"

"Yes, ma'am, but with good reason."

"Good reason? What could that possibly be?" Eilene's irate, high-pitched voice made Pam jump a little. She could definitely do without her mother's antics at the moment.

Vance stood up and joined her side.

Eilene sized up Vance before turning her focus back on her daughter.

"Well, I couldn't tell you all I was pregnant and about the possibility of Vance and me moving to Memphis. That was even too much for me to process at the same time."

"But you settled the fact that you all aren't moving, right?" Eilene craned her neck, rapidly blinking at Pam.

Pam stood silent.

Eilene's head snapped back. "Wh-what? You all *are* moving to Memphis? Away from me, your father, your brothers, and their families? The sisterhood? And with my grandchild?" Eilene braced her hand on the buffet table nearby and leaned over trying to steady her breath as if she were hyperventilating.

Pam looked back at her father and raised her hands in protest, begging him to help with her mother.

He merely shrugged his shoulders and slowly shook his head.

"Mom." Pam stepped forward and rubbed her mother's back. "Ma."

Eilene finally stood erect again. Her chest heaved as she stared at Pam. "You know my health problems. Are you trying to add a heart attack to them?"

Pam's brothers were busy being scolded by their father for laughing at their mother.

Vance stood not too far from Pam trying to calm his laughter. He'd had a front row seat many of times to Eilene's charades. And although he knew Pam hated the shows her mother put on, her antics never failed to entertain.

"Ma, I thought we got past all of these over the top dramatics. I thought you and I were in a better place."

"We are. That's why you can't move out of state. I can't imagine my life without you and Vance." She looked at him briefly. "And my grandchild. You would deny me the right to see him or her grow up? To hear them running through the house, calling me Nana just like the rest of my darlings."

"Ma," Pam said, moving closer to her and grabbing her hands into hers. "I love you, and I thank God for our relationship. No amount of distance will change that." She wiped at the tears on her mother's face. "And as for your grandchild, you won't miss out. I'll want you, need you there for the birth. You'll be at all of the birthday parties. We'll come back and visit as often as we can and you all can come visit when our schedules permit."

Pouting, Eilene grunted before pulling Pam into her embrace and squeezing her with all she had in her.

She soon pulled back with wide eyes. She looked down, placing her palms on Pam's belly.

She looked over Pam's shoulders and at her husband, "Tony, she has a nice sized pudge." She leaned over to be eye level with Pam's stomach. "She has a little pudge. Hello Nana's baby. I love you so much and I can't wait to meet you."

Smiling, she stood, cupped Pam's face, and kissed her cheek, before pulling her into another embrace. "Oh, you come here too." She motioned for Vance to join in the hugging fest.

He obliged and bent over to hug his much shorter wife and mother-in-law. Needing to stretch back out to his full height, he stood up and said to Pam, "You feel better?"

She nodded and wiped away her tears.

"Okay, well come back to the table and eat. You haven't eaten anything yet, and with the way you've been eating nonstop, I know you're starving."

She chuckled. "I sure am."

"Well get." Eilene shooed her to her seat and soon rejoined hers. She took a deep cleansing breath, but her eyes widened, looking up at Pam. "I'm going to try to get used to you no longer living in town, but what about the sisterhood? Have you told them?"

Pam dropped her fork and looked at her mom. "No."

"I'll pray for you on that one." Eilene shook her head with uncertainty. "You girls are definitely inseparable." Eilene began ranting as to how she envisioned Pam's baby shower.

Pam slowly chewed her food thinking about how she was going to break the news to Monica and Renee, and it had to be soon. The new school year had already started; she and Vance had to be in Memphis the next week.

23

Renee

Renee walked through her apartment's front door, dropped her bag, and trudged her way over to the sofa before falling face first on it.

She laughed at herself for her on-the-go-living-out-her-suitcase lifestyle she'd obtained over the past month or so.

In trying to bond with her son, she split her week between D.C. and Chicago. She worked twelve to sixteen-hour days Mondays through Thursdays, managing those under her, making house visits when needed, and doing paperwork. On Fridays, she caught the redeye to D.C. to resume her life with Isaiah.

Leaving early on Fridays left her room for any flight delays and the chance to sneak in a few hours of sleep before she headed to his Friday night games.

She attended his practices and games on Saturdays and ended by treating him to dinner. Grateful that Kristen and Josh had raised him up in a God-fearing way, she attended church with them on Sundays then helped him with his homework before she caught the last flight out on Sunday nights back to Chicago to start her tiring cycle all over again on Monday mornings.

She'd been doing that for over a month and although it made sense to her at first since he had taken a liking to her and she wanted to spend as much time with him as she could, weeks later, she knew she couldn't keep going as is. She just needed the courage to tell everyone the decision she'd made.

***

"Drew, where are you taking me?" Renee asked as she leaned back into his heated leather passenger seat.

"It wouldn't be a surprise if I told you." He smiled catching a glimpse of her before he pulled off from the entrance of her office building and into traffic.

"But I'm tired. Can't we do this another day?" Her head fell to the side, staring at him.

"You're always tired. We'd never do anything if that's the case."

"I'm sorry." She lifted her hand to caress his smooth chin. She smiled relishing in how handsome he was. "I know this past month has probably been a strain on our relationship. You trying to be there with me has you hopping flights even uncharacteristic for your busy schedule."

"I was out there with you from the beginning, but you know why I make it my business to be there even more so now."

Sitting up in her seat, she said, "I told you I don't think he'll bother me anymore."

"I told you I'm not taking any chances where you're concerned."

"Thank you." She smiled. "Okay, the night is yours. Ours. So where are we going?" She perked up in her seat.

He chuckled. "Still not telling you since it's a surprise." He turned up the Mali Music track and they rode in beautiful silence until he put his car in park and turned off the ignition.

Renee looked to her right and then back at him. "Drew, my parent's house is the surprise? What are we doing here?"

"You'll find out soon enough." He winked and rushed out the car to open her door.

After he opened the door, she took his proffered hand and allowed him to lead her to the front door.

While she was rummaging through her purse looking for her key to her parents' house, the door opened.

"Mom, how'd you know I was out here?"

"I didn't. I just so happened to be walking past the window and I saw you all out here." Mrs. Williams said, staring at Andrew.

"Thanks." He mouthed to her behind Renee.

"Okay. Well, sorry to bother you and Dad, but apparently Drew has a surprise here for me, or is this just a stop on the way to my surprise?" She looked back at him.

"Hi, Mrs. Williams." Andrew ushered Renee in the house and then brushed past her to hug Mrs. Williams.

"Everybody's here," she whispered in his ear.

"Great," He whispered before pulling away from her.

"Where's dad?" Renee asked, staring into the dark of the house.

"He's in the kitchen." Mrs. Williams rushed off.

Renee's eyes shifted to Andrew. "Really, what are we doing here?"

"I, we just needed to stop by and talk to your dad for a second."

"And then we'll get to my surprise?" Dating Andrew was like a constant cyclone of butterflies flapping in her stomach.

"Yes." He pulled her in for a quick, endearing kiss.

Her eyes fluttered as she pulled away from him. "Drew, not in my parents' house."

"It was just a quick kiss. Come on, let's go see your dad." He locked hands with her and pulled her towards the dark kitchen.

"Mom, I thought you went in the kitchen where you said Dad was. Where are you?" Renee said as Andrew's feet crossed the kitchen's threshold first. "Drew, let me turn the light on." She tried to pull away from him, but the darkness was suddenly replaced with the recessed lighting in the kitchen.

Her eyes adjusted to see her close-knit Chicago family around her. Monica was there with Keith, Pam and Vance, and of course her mother and father.

"Mom, Dad, what is going on?" Renee asked, looking to her parents.

On Andrew's cue, Monica adjusted the volume on the sound bar near her and Faith Evans *Never Gonna Let You Go* intro began to play.

Renee's eyebrows furrowed as she looked at Monica. "I've never heard that song before, but it sounds like R&B. Girl, you know you can't play that in here. You better put The Clark Sisters on before

Momma says something. And why were y'all just in the dark before the light came on all of sudden?" Renee looked at Keith shaking his head. "What, Keith? You know Momma never let us play secular music growing up."

"Renee, look at me."

"What, Drew?" She had been so focused on looking at everyone else to see why no one else saw anything wrong with the song playing that she hadn't even seen Andrew drop to one knee.

Feeling the tug on her hand, she finally looked down to see him. Her eyes widened. "Drew." Her hand flew up to her mouth. The song choice, the bouquet of flowers on the kitchen table, everyone at her parents' house on a Thursday night was making a little more sense to her. The singer's smooth yet soulful voice declaring never letting her lover go was making what was happening around her just a little clearer.

He smiled, staring at the unshed tears pooling her eyes and feeling the trembling of her hand. "Renee, I knew from the moment that I saw you in that hallway at my best friend, Kyle's wedding that there was something special about you. You grabbed a hold of my heart that day and I didn't even know it. This time we've spent getting to know one another has meant so much to me. You've changed me for the better, helped me to see life through a different lens, helped me to get closer to God, and I'm so thankful for that. You mean so much to me and just like the songs says, I'll never let you go. I wanna make us official." He caressed her trembling hand.

"Renee Katrina Williams, will you do me the honor of making me the happiest man on earth by becoming my wife? Will you marry me?"

She looked up at Keith hugging Monica as she cried, Vance rubbing Pam's shoulders as she bawled her eyes out, probably emotional from her pregnancy and the moment, and at her mother and father as he stood there with his chest out like a peacock and her mother dabbing at her eyes with a napkin.

"Renee, will you?" Andrew's tender plea pulled her attention back to him.

"Drew, I-I-I—"

He stood to his feet, wrapped his arm around her waist, and pulled her closer to him. "You what, baby?" No one could miss the alarm in his voice.

"Drew, I don't think you want to marry me."

"Yes, I do. There's nothing else I'd rather do." His big, expressive eyes begged her to trust him. When she didn't say anything, he asked, "Why would you think I don't want to marry you?"

"Because I'm moving to D.C.," she blurted out.

"What?" Monica shouted, moving closer to Renee.

"Hunh, baby?" Renee's father asked, drawing closer to her. His wife soon joined his side.

Renee pulled away from Andrew. She needed space to speak.

"I'm sorry you guys, but I can't do this anymore."

"Do what?" her mother asked.

"I can't keep up with this traveling back and forth like I have." Tears streamed her face. She cleared her throat to speak through her frustration of probably letting everyone down. "You all, I am so grateful to God that he gave my son a forgiving heart and has allowed me to be in his life. I've wanted this for so long. I've missed so many years and moments of his life that I don't want to miss any more. I want to be there for him as much as the Browns will allow me to."

Andrew took a step towards her but she held her hand up. "You can't stop me, Drew, none of you all can. I had filled out an application to be a social worker there and was still contemplating the decision, but they just got back to me the other day saying I got the job. I took it as confirmation for me to move there." Her eyes were red as she looked around the room at everyone else. "I'm sorry for disappointing you all but—"

"Renee, you aren't disappointing me." Pam got up from her seat and walked over to Renee "I have a confession, too."

Everyone looked at her with raised eyebrows. "Vance accepted a leadership position in Memphis, and he and I will be moving there next week." Vance walked over to her and pulled her into him as she cried at her admission.

"No, no. You guys can't leave me," Monica said on a sob as she stepped closer to Pam and Renee. "Kim is already gone, I'll have no one here with me, with the babies." She dropped her head and her shoulders heaved up and down.

Pam and Renee walked up to her and the three shared a sorrow-filled embrace for quite some time.

Mrs. Williams soon joined the women, rubbing their backs and softly praying for them.

When their cries seemed to taper off, Keith walked up to Monica and pulled on her shoulder, coaxing her to face him. His finger hooked under her soft chin, forcing her to look up at him. "Mo, I'm sorry that I abandoned you for all of those months, had you handling everything on your own, but we're back on track. Please know that I'm here for you. I'll never neglect you again. You have me, you're not alone."

She gathered on her tip toes, threw her arms around his neck, and held on to him for dear life. Finally pulling away from him, she said, "Even when you were distant, I knew that we weren't done. I know you'll always be here for me, but they are my girls, my sisters." She hiccupped through a cry.

He pulled her into him and rubbed her back.

Renee turned to Pam. "You're moving away, too? Here I was thinking that my announcement would be such a shock leaving you two behind but you were gonna leave us?"

Pam threw her arms around Renee. "I'm sorry. I fought not going until the end." She pulled away from Renee and looked between Renee and Monica as Monica approached them. "But I realized that my decision to stay here and not to break up the rest of the sisterhood was mine alone. I was being selfish and not thinking about what was best for my husband, for our growing family."

"Ugh, you two make me sick." Monica laughed through a cry pulling them in for another hug. She kissed both of their cheeks before pulling away from them. They locked hands with one another, standing in a circle. "We've been through so much this past year, you guys. Can we really survive these moves? Always sisters, always friends?" She sang the last of her words.

Pam reached up and wiped the tears on Monica's face.

"Look at all we've been through over the years—abortions, secret adoptions, abusive boyfriends, marital affairs, cancer, and the death of our sister and best friend, and we're still here for each other. We're still standing." They looked at their interlaced hands and squeezed each other's tighter. "God has us. I'm convinced nothing will ever tear us apart," Pam said.

Renee shook her head. "I don't know why I was worried. The Bible says take no thought for tomorrow, to be anxious for nothing but by prayer and supplication, make our requests known to him. I should've known that after all of the years of praying to meet my son and it finally manifesting that God would work things out and bless us to keep our bond strong, no matter which way life takes us.

"And Pam is right, we're stuck with each other and that's a good thing." She smiled, causing the others to laugh. "We may not see each other as often as we'd like, but we'll keep up with our phone chats and we can plan quarterly face-to-face visits."

Monica heaved a heavy breath. "But our babies won't grow up together."

"Yes, they will," Renee exclaimed.

"Between the visits and face-time, the twins will know their auntie Renee and my baby will know his or her big cousins and aunties Monica and Renee. They'll know how much their Auntie Kim loved them, too." Pam rubbed her stomach.

Monica pouted. "You all are right. With time comes change and although I don't like the changes the physical distance between us will cause, I love you all and I'm committed to making this all work. I don't want new friends, you all."

"What?" Renee asked, confused.

"I'm serious. I don't want new friends. You hear that Keith?" She turned to face him, "You better prepare for me to be all up in your face. I'm too old to be making new friends, besides, I love the ones I already have too much to break some new ones in."

Everyone in the kitchen laughed, except for Andrew who stood by silent waiting for the sisterhood to finish their moment so that he could get back to his. Thankfully, he knew the time they were using to air things out was needed.

Keith shook his head. "I got you, baby, but you know you've taken a liking to Vance's brother's wife and his friend Anthony's wife."

Monica scrunched her face up. "Yeah, you're right, but still they aren't Renee and Pam. And no one, I mean no one, will ever be able to replace Kim."

A contemplative silence fell over the kitchen for a bit.

Renee was the first to speak up, "So, we're good?" She looked to Monica and Pam.

"Of course."

"Yes."

Monica and Pam said respectively.

They stepped into another hug. Renee pulled away from them and turned to her parents. "Mom,

Dad, I'm sorry for not telling you sooner, but I have to make this move."

Her mother pulled her into the warmest embrace she had yet to experience. It made her want to cry, yet it brought so much comfort to her that all she could do was smile, close her eyes, and take in her mother's soothing scent.

"Baby, there's nothing you could ever do to make us stop loving you. We raised you to be the strong woman you've grown into. We love you so much." Her mother kissed her temple.

Her father walked closer to them and wrapped his arm around her, leaned into her and said, "I can't lie and say I won't miss you, but you go up there and take care of my grandson, you hear me?"

"Oh, I love you too, Daddy." She turned and flung her arms over her daddy, hugging him with all she had in her.

The loud clearing of a throat forced Mr. Williams to speak. "I think someone is trying to get your attention."

Renee pulled away from her father and wiped her face as she turned to face Andrew. So much time had elapsed since he asked her to marry him, that she wondered if he even still wanted to.

The butterflies she always felt when she was around him, talked to him, or thought about him returned as they made advancing steps towards one another. "Drew, I'm sorry I didn't give you the answer you wanted." She took a deep breath believing her next words might be the last ones she ever spoke to him. "I just think it's best if we end things now. I love you too much to tie you up in a long-distance relationship."

He shook his head as he wrapped his arm around her waist and pulled her into him. "Renee?"

Holding her breath, not knowing what would happen next for them, she looked up at him. "Hunh?"

He said nothing but responded with his lips melded against hers. Never kissing a man before in front of her parents, she tried to push him away from her, but he planted his free hand in her hair and tilted her head to gain greater access to her mouth.

Remembering that she was grown and thinking that it might actually be the last kiss with the man she loved, she grabbed a hold of him and deepened their kiss.

"A-hem." Mr. Williams's deep voice rose above the song on loop filtering throughout the kitchen.

Renee pulled her lips away from Andrew only when she'd had her fill of his taste. They rested their foreheads on one another.

Mr. Williams cleared his throat again.

Laughing, Mrs. Williams swatted at her husband. "Tyrone, leave them alone. They are grown."

He frowned looking at his wife. "She's still my baby. I've never seen her like this before." He grunted.

"So, what. Andrew already asked you for her hand in marriage. You knew this was coming."

"Still doesn't mean I have to like it." He pouted a little longer before he pulled his wife into his side and planted a kiss on her cheek.

"I guess this is goodbye, hunh?" Renee said, hesitantly trying to pull away from Andrew.

He shook his head and kept his possessive, yet gentle hold of her lean frame. "You really don't listen, do you? I just told you that I'm never letting you go. I picked this song to help tell you how I feel." He gripped her chin, forcing her to look him directly in his eyes. "I'm never letting you go." The emotions lodged in his throat made his voice raspy.

"But I'm moving to another state. Chicago is home for you."

"Renee, I live out of a suitcase traveling across the country. Look how much I've been in D.C. with you. My home is where you are." He tightened his grip around her waist with one hand and caressed her face with his other.

She closed her eyes and took a deep breath, treasuring his touch, his presence. When she opened them, her dark brown eyes stared into his and she said, "So you'd move to D.C. with me?"

"I'll go anywhere you go, Renee. Home is where the heart is and my heart is with you." He released his hold on her and dropped to one knee in front of her again. "Renee Katrina Williams, again I ask you, will you do me the honor of being my wife?"

Smiling, she stared at him through her tears. "Yes, Drew, I'll marry you."

He took the custom designed ring he had made from the black box he'd been holding on to since they first entered the kitchen. It looked like an antique, a family heirloom of some sort and he smiled as he placed it on her finger.

She didn't even bother looking at it but rather jumped up and down a little, holding her arms out, waiting for him to stand and embrace her.

Everyone else in the room cheered them on.

Their celebratory kiss was interrupted by her mother coming to them and pulling Renee away to embrace and congratulate her.

"Thank you, Mom," Renee said, smiling and crying.

Pam and Monica were soon by her side. "I'm so happy for you two," Monica said, hugging Renee and looking at Andrew.

"Thanks," he said to Monica and Pam after their congratulations.

"I guess it's an official welcome to the family moment, hunh?" Keith said, standing next to Andrew.

Mr. Williams came up and flanked the other side of Andrew.

"So you know to always treat her right, right?" Mr. Williams said, peering down at Andrew.

Andrew looked to his left to see Keith holding the same defensive stance and stoic face as his father. Andrew laughed. "Of course, gentleman. She's as much my gift as she is a treasure to you all. She's been your princess, Mr. Williams, but she'll be my queen."

Mr. Williams could only nod his head at such a statement.

Keith wasn't so moved by the eloquence of his words. "Yeah, you just better remember how a queen is supposed to be treated at all times."

"Keith, I thought we got past this hump already," Andrew said, gauging Keith's demeanor.

Keith broke out laughing and the exchange went unnoticed between the women in the room still gushing over Renee.

"Are you always gonna be like this with me?" Andrew asked, accepting Keith's one-armed hug.

"Naw, I'm done with the act now. You're good for my sister. Welcome to the family. You've got a special woman on your hands there," Keith said, nodding his head towards Renee.

"I know I do," Andrew said, beaming and staring at Renee.

They locked eyes and it was like a big magnet pulling them together. The others stepped aside to allow them to embrace again.

"I love you," Renee said into his ear.

"I love you more." He pulled back from her just enough to press his lips to hers.

"Okay, enough with that, we have a wedding to plan. Gosh, this is going to be hard with busy toddlers, demanding newborns, and you two away in different states," Monica said, walking up to Andrew and Renee.

"What?" Renee looked wide eyed at Monica. "You know, I've never wanted a big fancy wedding."

"I know, but you're the last one to get married and since Pam eloped and Kim…" She let her words trail off but plastered a smile on her face to keep the moment joyous. "You have to have a big wedding."

"You covered that with your extravagant wedding with Keith," Pam said not too far away from the ladies.

"Ugh, you all are determined to make my life less exciting."

Just then the twins' cries could be heard through the monitors.

"I don't see how you could ever claim your life is not exciting with two sets of twins." Her father-in-law chided her.

"Don't worry, Monica. Tyrone and I will go and see about them. Come on grandpa." Roberta looked to her husband.

"Thanks Mom, but those cries require these." She pointed to her breasts. Mrs. Williams laughed but Mr. Williams held his hands up in surrender and stepped back.

"Come on daddy-o," Monica said, looking at Keith.

"Well, we'll go see about the other set then. Come on Grandpa. We're still needed." Roberta smiled at her husband as they walked hand in hand down the hall and headed to the nursery they'd created.

"Aw, again, congratulations, Renee. I'm so happy for you. You deserve nothing but the best." Pam hugged Renee.

"Thank you. You, too." Renee pulled back from Pam and rubbed her belly. "Oh my gosh, it's still surreal that you're pregnant." She reached in to hug Pam again.

"Okay, I really do love you guys and am so happy for you all, but I am really, really hungry. There are some pineapples waiting on meat the house."

Vance shook his head as he grabbed their jackets from off the back of a chair at the table.

Pam whipped around at Vance. "Don't forget that we have to go out west to Jimmy's on Pulaski and

Grand. I have to get a polish and fries from there, maybe two."

Vance came up behind her and motioned for her to put her arms into the jacket. She obliged him all the while talking. "And while we're out, we might as well swing by Uncle Remus lon Madison and Central. I'll get a grab pan of their fried chicken drenched in their yummy mild sauce. What are you eating tonight?" She looked over her shoulder at him.

"Whatever, it doesn't matter to me." He chuckled and rushed to Andrew to engage him in a one-armed hug. "Congrats, bro. Let me get her out of here before she has me stopping by a million more restaurants before we ever make it home. Congrats, Renee." He leaned in and kissed her on her jaw and then pulled Pam by her arm as she continued on about all she had a taste for.

When they heard the front door close, Renee briefly looked at her ring and then up at Andrew. "So, we're really getting married?" Her pert mouth curved into an infectious smile.

"As long as I have a say so, yes, my love, we're getting married," he said, pulling her into him.

With her body colliding into his solid frame, she let out a small yelp, delighting in the moment.

"You've barely looked at your ring. How will you know if you like it or not? If I should get you another one?"

She pecked his nose with her index finger. "You know I'm not into material things." She lifted her left hand eye level and her eyes widened and her pupils dilated staring at the ring's magnificence.

He smiled watching her.

She finally pulled her eyes away from the ring to gaze into his eyes. "It is absolutely gorgeous. In fact, it reminds me of a ring they have at that antique shop we visited in D.C."

"I know." Andrew winked.

"What? How'd you know?"

"Because, I pay attention to you. You don't like flashy, you like meaningful. As many times as you've talked about visiting that shop while you were there, one day when I came in to see you, I swung by it in hopes of finding a ring there that you might like. They had one, but I didn't think it was good enough for you, but I bought it anyway. I took it to a jeweler, recommended by a client of mine, and they designed yours based on the one I got from the shop."

She pecked his lips. "You are so good to me."

"And you are so good for me."

His full, firm lips covered hers as he explored her mouth with a patience that said his heart really did belong to her.

Renee kissed him back mirroring the same sentiment.

24

Darius

He pulled the door open at the same time she pushed on it with her hip, staring at her phone screen in her hand.

"I'm sorry. Forgive me for not watching where I was going." She looked up to see who had stopped her from toppling over. "Darius." Her eyes locked with his.

"Dr. Wyndham."

Unnerved by the intense way he stared at her, she stepped back from him and smoothed her skirt and her hair down.

He realized he'd been staring at her for far too long without saying something. He cleared the desire for her from his throat long enough to say, "Headed home?" he asked, rubbing the back of his head, unsure of the plan he'd set out to execute.

"Yeah, it's been a long day."

"Too tired to go somewhere and talk for a second?" He massaged his neck, awaiting her response.

"No. Have a place in mind?"

"I saw a café not too far up the street, but if you're hungry and would prefer an actual meal, I can look up a place nearby. Unless you know of a restaurant around you'd like to go to?"

"No, the café is just fine."

"Here, let me grab your bag for you." He gripped her briefcase and their hands touched as she looked up at him for a second, unsure if he'd felt what she did when his hand touched hers.

"I have it," she said in a wispy breath.

"No, let me get it, please?"

She acquiesced and he stepped aside to let her pass out onto the street.

She buttoned up the top button of her heather gray pea coat.

"It's brisk out here isn't it?" He chuckled, trying to release his nervous energy.

"Yeah, Chicago seasons are always so unpredictable. You'd think it was the end of fall rather than it barely starting."

"Right. Taking this to your car or are we headed straight to the café?" he asked, holding up her briefcase as a reference.

"We can go straight there."

"Not gonna change your shoes?" He looked down at her smooth stride in what he assumed had to be at least six-inch heels.

She kicked one leg up twisting her foot in the air from side to side. "These are like gym shoes to me." Smirking, she looked over at him.

"Excuse me." He feigned taking offense to her declaration.

An odd silence enveloped them as they walked a few doors over to the café. Once inside, he guided her to a seat in the back, took her order, and placed it before returning to the table.

He sat in the booth across from her. "They said they'll bring our orders to the table as soon as they're ready. Sorry, was that your knee?" he asked after bumping his into hers.

"Yeah, but don't worry about it." She offered up a half-smile. "So, what brought you to my office tonight, Darius?" She sat up straight, adjusting her cobalt blue blazer, before fixing her professional stare on him.

He shifted in his seat. "Wow, straight to the punch line." He looked away, rubbing his jaw. "Well, we were talking often and then you stopped answering my calls, no more sessions. You just vanished on me. Even a stop by the office went unanswered by you."

"I apologize for terminating our sessions without the proper notice." Her voice was even, unlike the mix of emotions broiling in her stomach.

"Why though? I told you how you'd be helping me fair after losing Kim. You said I was making great progress." He laughed.

Unsure of what prompted his chuckle at that juncture of their conversation, she spoke up, "Something funny?"

"Sorry, not necessarily funny, but in trying to make sense of why we stopped talking, I just thought about something my homeboys said to me."

She wasn't one to pry into a person's personal life and only asked her patients personal questions when the answer might be necessary to their evolution. She initially thought not to dig into what Darius found funny, but he was no longer her patient, and well, curiosity had gotten the best of her. "Which is?" She rolled her hand in the air, beckoning him to carry on.

"Again, no punches, I see. Well, when I told them how I was doing because of your expertise and our interactions, they said you probably stopped talking to me because you wanted us to be more than friends."

"Thank you." She offered the quick response to the server as he placed her tray in front of her and then Darius's tray in front of him.

"Thanks, man," Darius said, barely looking at the young man. "But I was thinking it was maybe because

I did something wrong, talked to you too often, or didn't pay you enough money." He laughed and scanned his salad making sure it was the exact way he ordered it.

She never joined in laughing.

Not hearing her melodic laugh, he looked up and noted the look on her face. It forced him to sit up erect. "Their assumption was incorrect, right?"

"Let me preface my answer by saying that I've never had this problem with a patient before. I pride myself on being professional at all times. I never cross the line, but with you, I fell face first over it."

Stunned by her admission, Darius pushed his plate away from him and anchored his forearms on the table.

She shook her head looking at him. "I knew there was something special about you from the moment I met you, but given the reason we met, I knew my feelings didn't matter."

"Wow. Why didn't you ever say anything?"

"What would it have mattered?" she blurted out. She took a deep breath. "You came to me to help you deal with your grief over the loss of a girlfriend, and I fell for you. That's a recipe for disaster. You said so yourself, you didn't know if you'd ever love again. So why would I open up to you about how I felt only to be smacked in the face with a reality I already knew."

He sat silent and she felt the need to better explain herself, recover some of the dignity she'd felt she lost telling a former patient she wanted him. "Every time we had a session on the phone or via video, I left them knowing I should've referred you to someone else, but my heart begged me for more encounters with you. You made me laugh like never before. I saw how charismatic you are, smart, driven. I know I was wrong for the way I ended our working relationship, but it was the only way I thought to handle my feelings for you at the time, to completely cut you off."

Taken aback, he sat quiet for a second.

She knew her confession may have been out of the blue and heavy depending on how one looked at it but him saying nothing was too much for her. The way he told jokes back to back and even the way he opened up to her during his sessions, she knew he was hardly ever at a loss for words. *No, I just put my foot knee deep into my mouth, and I should just leave now.*

"Bye, Darius." She grabbed her purse from the spot next to her and attempted to get up from the table, but his hand on hers and his voice stopped her from leaving.

She barely looked at him as she sat back in her space.

"I'm sorry for being so tongue-tied, but I'm trying to choose my words carefully."

"You know what? You don't have to say a thing. Again, I apologize for the abrupt way I ended our sessions and allowing my assistant to end our professional relationship rather than doing it myself. If you need me to, I can refer you to another counselor if you're still in need of one, but if not, I'm glad you're doing better and I wish you the best of luck moving forward."

"Dr. Wyndham, wait, don't go." He watched her adjust her purse on her lap and finally look at him, letting him know he still had her attention. "You keep saying our sessions as if that's all they were. Yeah, I was your patient being billed for you expertise, but I honestly had come to look at you like a friend and enjoyed our chats. Had I been in Chicago more often, I would've insisted we hung out outside of our sessions. I really do see you as a good friend. You're right, at one point, I did say I'd never love again, but you helped me to see that I can when I'm ready. I'm not ready to date anyone, but I'm not ready to lose you as a friend either."

"It's good that you're aware of your feelings and know what you do and don't want, but because I am too, I know we can't be friends. Good bye, Darius." This time she left the table with no protest from him.

He slapped the table after he lost sight of her through the café window. "Damn, why do I keep losing the ones I really cares about?"

25

Renee

Rain pellets hit the car as it pulled up to the side of the thick tree trunk. "You ready to do this?" Renee's father asked as he sat across from her in the back of the extravagant car.

"Yes, Daddy." She smiled looking at her father and then at her mother seated next to him.

"Monica, was this limo really necessary? I could've just drove my car," Renee said, staring at her.

"Yes, it was necessary. This may not be a grand wedding in a beautiful banquet hall, but you could at least still ride to your ceremony in style."

"I have to agree with Monica. The limo is a nice touch," Pam said.

"I'm just glad we decided to do this before you and Vance moved," Renee said.

"Even if we would've left, you know I would've come back. I wouldn't have missed this day for anything in the world," Pam remarked.

"Aww, don't cry," Monica said as she leaned in to hug Renee, and Pam did the same on the other side of Renee.

"I love you all so much," Renee uttered.

"And we love you, too," Monica said.

"Now stop crying before you look like a raccoon and mess up your pretty face. You know Kim would have a fit if she saw you looking so pretty but letting your tears ruin your make up," Pam said.

"And you know she would have a fit if she saw this dress, boot combo. Really? We left you alone in your apartment for five minutes and you come down to the car with galoshes on? What happened to the shoes we picked out to go with the dress?" Monica laughed.

Everyone laughed in the car.

"What? I knew I had to walk in that dirt out there. I'm already pushing it with this dress." She looked down at herself. "The shoes are more my style and their comfy. Besides, I probably would've fell over in those heels of Kim's."

"Well, Andrew is gonna fall over when he sees you in this dress," Monica said.

Renee pulled on the hem of the dress trying to pull it closer to her knees. "It's too tight, isn't it?" She frowned.

"Renee, it's your birthday and your wedding day. Live a little. And you look smoking hot in it." Monica winked.

"Okay, baby girl, everyone's waiting on you," Mr. Williams said.

"Your father's right. Let's go," her mother said as she leaned to open the car door. She soon stepped out followed by Pam and Monica in their cute, knee-length bridesmaid's dresses. Mrs. Williams walked ahead and mindlessly rubbed Kim's headstone as she chatted with their pastor who was there to officiate the wedding.

Pam and Monica stood in front of the car door as if to provide one last buffer to keep everyone from seeing Renee before it was her time to make her way to her groom.

Renee sat in the car a little longer staring through the rain at those near Kim's headstone.

Andrew stood as handsome as ever directly to the left of the stone with his best friend, Kyle Irving, not too far from him. She smiled seeing Andrew's adoptive family as well as his birth mother Marie and his biological sister, Melanie, who was standing next to her best friend and Kyle's wife, Karen.

A thick canopy of trees seemed to shield everyone ahead of her from the rain. They didn't even need to hold the umbrellas they held down at their sides.

On what may have been considered her side of the odd venue, it warmed her heart to see Vance, his friends and their wives, except for Darius. He was nowhere in sight.

She smiled wide seeing her coworker, Amina present. She could see Amina's elation for her given the wide smile on her face.

She had to stop herself from crying when she laid eyes on the Browns. Even with such short notice, they had brought Isaiah to the wedding and to meet the rest of his family.

While she could've pretended like everyone had come out to celebrate her nuptials to Andrew, it being her, Keith, and Kim's birthday as well helped to solidify her guest list, given the venue.

Although morbid to outsiders, Renee and Andrew decided to have their intimate wedding ceremony at a Kim's burial site. They wanted her somehow included in the day.

Everyone stood in support of their decision to commemorate a life and to celebrate the occasion.

Renee took a deep breath and accepted her father's hand as he helped her from the car. She was immediately covered by an umbrella Keith was holding. It definitely shielded her from the steady flow of rain. She looked up at him and smiled before reaching on her tip toes to kiss him on his cheek. "I love you, too."

They held hands and as if instinctively, their attention was drawn to Kim's headstone where they laid eyes on her infectious smile etched in the stone. It was like she was smiling directly at them.

They looked at each other at the same time. "She's smiling at us," Renee said, no longer containing her tears.

"I know. She's saying live, too," Keith said, reaching down and hugging his sister with all he had in him. He pulled back from her and wiped her face. They found themselves looking at the stone one last time together and it was like the power of all three of their smiles made the rain stop and the sun peaked through a few clouds, just enough to lighten up the rather cloudy day.

Keith dropped the umbrella to the ground and held his hand out to help his sister step over the water puddle at her feet. He looked down and shook his head, "Really, Renee? Even I know those rain boots don't match that dress peaking from under your raincoat."

"Leave me alone." She laughed. "Take my coat, will you?"

"You sure? Yeah, the sun is out a little, but it's still fall and this wind ain't the friendliest."

"I'll be fine, brother."

"Okay." He pulled her coat off her but when he saw how fitted her dress was, he threw it back over her. "Nah, I think you'll be better with it on."

"Keith, stop playing," Monica mouthed through tight lips not too far from them.

"Ugh, y'all doing too much. She would've looked just fine in one of those long skirts and plaid shirts she normally wears."

"Keith," Renee exclaimed.

"Okay. Okay. Okay." He laughed and pulled the coat from her again and threw it through the open car door.

"Daddy." Renee looked over to her father with her elbow out.

He locked his arm with hers and kissed her cheek.

"Monica," Renee whispered, letting her know to begin the ceremony.

Vance walked arm and arm with Pam down the makeshift aisle patterned with leaves and then Keith and Monica followed a few paces behind them.

When they had taken their places near to where Renee and Andrew would exchange their vows, Andrew had an unobstructed view of Renee readying to walk towards him.

She was a sight to behold.

Although no music was playing, Renee and her father marched along the path of leaves as if she had a full band playing the wedding song for her.

While everyone chuckled at the rhythmless Renee bob down the aisle, Andrew could only marvel at his queen making her way to him.

He knew clothes didn't make a person, but the only word that played over and over in his mind as he stared at Renee was an expletive better left unsaid. He'd discuss the form fitting bandage dress with her later.

Renee smiled at Andrew's expression as her father turned her hand over to him. The cream bandage bodycon dress she was wearing fit her like a second skin. Oddly, she didn't look uncomfortable in it like he imagined she would in clothes outside of her lose fitted clothing and ankle length skirts she always wore.

She whispered to him, "You like?"

"What do you think?" Andrew smirked. He was beside himself, taking in her dress. Before his thoughts could really get away from him, the pastor's voice redirected his attention.

"We're gathered here today at what some might consider an odd place to get married but who cares what they think."

"Amen," a few called out from among the crowd.

"This is a great memorial for the late Kimberly Denise Williams."

Mrs. Williams wiped her face and Mr. Williams rubbed her back.

"The couple has decided to write their own vows. Andrew, you first."

"Renee…" He carried on confessing his love for her before he almost choked on the sentiments in his throat as he ended his vows. He smiled and kissed her hand.

Her face was soaked with tears by the time he finished his serenade of heart-string pulling words to her.

"Drew, I wrote out a long letter of how I really feel about you, but after what you just said, I just want to speak from my heart right now. Loving you has been a journey for me. You know my past and because of it I felt ashamed for a long time, but you've always embraced me as is. You never made fun of my long skirts and always caught me when I tripped over the hem."

Their audience laughed at that admission.

Out of the corner of her eye, Renee caught Darius walk up and kiss her mother on her cheek before he stepped back next to Marcus and Anthony. She turned her attention back to the handsome groom in front of her and continued her ode to him, "You just love me for me and I love that. You are an amazing man, so full of life and valor. You're honest and brave and I always want to be by your side, growing through life with you. I promise to love you every day of my life." The last of her words left her choked up and in definite need of the tissue Pam passed her.

"Well, I don't see how there can be a dry eye after that," Pastor Johnson said and many of the women laughed, dabbing their tears away. "The rings please."

Monica stepped forward and grabbed Renee's bouquet and then Pam handed her the ring for Andrew.

Kyle tapped Andrew on the arm and handed him the ring he was holding.

"Grab each other's hands." The pastor commanded. When satisfied that they had followed his directions, he said, "Repeat after me. With this ring."

"With this ring," Andrew and Renee said in unison.

"I thee wed."

"I thee wed."

He gave them a moment to fully slide the rings on each other's fingers.

The act garnered high wattage smiles from the duo.

"By the powers vested in me by the City of Chicago, I now pronounce you husband and wife. You may kiss your bride."

The words barely left the pastor's lips before Andrew snatched Renee up and kissed her like he never had before.

Renee soon pulled away from him, heaving and patting her lips, wondering if they were swollen.

He laughed at her. "They're fine." He leaned down and placed a gentler kiss to her lips. "Better?"

"A little," she said before pulling him in for one more kiss.

"Okay you two. Let's do the other part of this ceremony while the weather is cooperating with us," Mrs. Williams said.

"Actually Ma, we can't do what I originally planned with the balloon release. It's cold outside to the point where the balloons wouldn't fly, so we got loads of bouquets to lay around her grave," Monica said.

Mrs. Williams yelped a sob as she saw Vance and his friends reemerge from a car with their arms filled with tons of flowers. They handed them out to everyone in attendance and they all took their turn at Kim's headstone, lingering there for a moment of silence and then they each handed one long-stemmed flower to Renee. She would leave with a bouquet arranged by everyone in attendance, sort of like a binding moment for everyone.

When Isaiah made his way to drop his flowers, she rubbed his head and smiled down at him. "I wish you would've met her."

"Me, too," he said as he dropped his flowers, handed Renee one, and then hugged her. His parents were right behind him following suit and then hugged Renee. "We're so happy for you and we'll see you soon at the reception."

"Okay. Again, thank you all so much for letting me into his life and for bringing him here today for this special moment in my life." Renee's tears danced on her face.

"Don't cry." Kristen patted Renee's arm. "We told you we knew the day could come. We're just grateful that it was you who showed up at our door and not some crazy woman demanding to see him."

Renee laughed. "Right." She watched them leave and when she looked around her, everyone had gone to their cars. It was just her and Andrew standing in front of Kim's headstone.

He braced his arm around her and pulled her free hand up to his lips.

"You okay?" he asked.

"Yeah, just looking at that smile of hers and remembering the times we shared. I wish she could've been here today when we said I do."

"She may not have been here physically, but she was and will always be here." He pointed to the center of her chest.

"You're right." She looked over and kissed him again.

"Now about this dress." He twirled her around with her hand he was holding.

She giggled. "It's actually one of Kim's dresses. She used to try and get me to put it on all the time. I know she'd be delighted that I finally decided to wear it, but I'm glad you're pleased with it."

"Babe, I love you in it, but I can't wait to see you out of it."

"Drew." She hit him on his chest as they walked towards the car with his arm wrapped around her.

"What? We're married now. You're fair game, baby." He paused their steps, cupped her chin, and looked into her eyes before engaging her in a kiss that shook her core.

"Come on. Let's go celebrate our love and you alls birthday with everyone."

"Let's." She smiled as they walked back to the car hand in hand.

"You straight?" Vance asked Darius as he, Anthony, and Marcus stood around him.

"Yeah."

"We didn't think you were coming," Marcus said.

"I wasn't at first. Thought being here would take me back to the dark moments right after she passed, but when I got here and saw her beautiful face etched on her headstone, I felt at peace."

"Good, man," Anthony said.

"Yeah, she'll always be in my heart, but loving her taught me that I can love again." Darius smiled.

"That's definitely the best way to look at life. So, you going to the reception?" Vance said.

"Yeah, I'll meet y'all over there, but I need to make a call first." He walked over to his car as they walked to theirs.

When he was settled in his car, he pressed two, causing his phone to speed dial Dr. Wyndham. Surprisingly, she picked up. "Danielle?"

"Yes, Darius?"

"With all things considered, you willing to start from scratch with me?"

Other Books Available

Sisterhood Chronicles Series
Underneath It All
Discovery
Untold
When It Happens To You
All Things Considered

Forever Friends Series
Catch Me If You Can
It's Complicated

Limelight Series
Hues
Tones
Vision

Love Alive Series
The Kissing Game

Standalone Titles
After All Is Said & Done
The Bid Catcher: Distinguished Gentlemen Series

(Best if you read Forever Friends series before reading Sisterhood Chronicles 3)

ABOUT THE AUTHOR

Anita Davis is a former elementary teacher born and raised in Chicago. Although she wrote short stories much of her childhood, she didn't unlock and cultivate her passion as a writer until she became a writing teacher for middle school students. The more she had to create sample writings for her students, the more she realized her passion and ability to tell stories in the written form. She decided to hone her craft as a writer by completing her Master of Fine Arts in Creative Writing via National University. She now pursues writing books most of her time, in addition to being a flight attendant. Anita seeks to encourage, engage, and entertain her readers.

She is Co-Founder of Book Euphoria, a group of Chicago authors bound by their love of literature. Book Euphoria hosts literary events and they also founded the empowerment movement, Black Girl Passion.

Anita writes contemporary romantic women's fiction and seeks to encourage, engage, and entertain her readers.

authoranitadavis@gmail.com
www.authoranitadavis.com
Facebook: Anita Davis and Author page: Author Anita Davis
Instagram: @authoranitadavis   Twitter: @_AnitaDavis

www.ingramcontent.com/pod-product-compliance
Lightning Source LLC
Chambersburg PA
CBHW062127170626
46813CB00002B/602